Dwarf Stories

Other books by Bruce Lawder

Poetry

Little Choice
Shadings
Afterthoughts
Shorelines

Essays

Vers le vers

Dwarf Stories

Bruce Lawder

Homestead Lighthouse Press

Grants Pass, Oregon

Dwarf Stories copyright © Bruce Lawder, 2024, Homestead Lighthouse Press, First Edition

All rights reserved. No part of this book may be reproduced or transmitted in any form without the prior written permission of the publisher.

Library of Congress Cataloging-in-Publication Data Pending

Names: Bruce Lawder, author.

Library of Congress Control Number:

ISBN 978-1-950475-34-6

Homestead Lighthouse Press
1668 NE Foothill Boulevard
Unit A
Grants Pass, OR 97526
www.homesteadlighthousepress.com

Distributed by Homestead Lighthouse Press, Daedalus Distribution, Amazon.com, Barnes & Noble

Cover & Book Design: Ray Rhamey, Ashland, OR

Homestead Lighthouse Press gratefully acknowledges the generous support of its readers and patrons.

Contents

Acknowledgments

The following five stories originally appeared under the title of "Dwarf Stories" in *TriQuarterly*: "The New Laws," "The Competition," "This Will Be Yours," "Personal Objects," and "Saturn". "Monument to Fascism," "The Last Boat," and "Rain" were first published in *Little Star*; "Masks" in *The Massachusetts Review*; and "Memorial," "Guards and Prisoners," "Country of Bridges," "Sign and Signature," "The Dwarf," "Tomorrow and Tomorrow," and "The Stealing of the Law" in *Notre Dame Review*; "The Position," "All's Well," and "The Hunger Wall" first appeared in Web *Conjunctions*; "Cassandra" and "Black Fruit" in separate online editions of *Little Star*; "Knight," "Variations on a Theme," and "The Absconditen" on the web site of *Notre Dame Review*; "The Pillar," "The Empire of the Singers," and "The Statue" in *Agni*, and "The Summons" in *Bitter Oleander*.

I call these stories Dwarf Stories because,
for the most part, they are shorter than short.

For Gaby

The We People

From Here to There

It is important for us to get from here to there, that is simply the way it is, and once there, here, and here, there, and so here. So it goes, from here to there, or from there to here, so it has been going for years and so it is going to go. It is not what is there that is of interest there, what is there is much like what is here, and once there I for one turn my interest to what is here, as once here to what is there. That is simply the way it is. Business depends on these transactions, exports and imports would not be what they are without this movement, and it is the movement that is of interest, otherwise, exports and imports would not be what they are, and in exports and imports, there is no otherwise, only this movement from here to there, from there to here. "Here we are," we say and of course, it is too late. For what is here must be there, not here, what is there, if not here, is already underway.

Personal Objects

"Why has everything been destroyed?" I asked, new to the office and unable to understand how everyone could take everything so routinely.

"Everything has not been destroyed," my secretary answered, not without bitterness, it seemed to me. "Everything cannot be destroyed. Only personal objects." I looked around me and saw that indeed this was the case: plants, photographs, and even books had been stripped from the desks and walls and thrown onto the floor. But the machines were in order. The surfaces of the desks were empty and clean. "It is the Maintenance Department," she said. "It is only a matter of form, pure form, and nothing but form. The corporation does not own the air space, and there are insurance regulations to satisfy, that is the problem. At least, that is what I have been told. But I don't understand these things," she admitted, as if this, too, were of no interest to her, and began putting her things back in place. I turned to my own space, expecting chaos there, but found everything exactly as it had always been.

"That's because you have no personal objects," my secretary said. "That is the only way to defeat them. But then, of course, they have already won."

The Competition

From his sounds I know he is there, on the other side of the wall, all day I can hear him writing or talking, calling or being called, doing exactly what I do, even as I do it, but without complaint, for nothing appears to interrupt him, even the sounds of the city he pays no attention to, sounds I cannot bear, in particular the sounds of repairs, for me something like our national anthem, construction or deconstruction in an incessant if discontinuous single assault on our lives.

He is there, simply there, an immigrant, a man of my age, as my grandfather was, a foreigner who has not even mastered the language, from what I can hear, yet language is no longer of the first importance, if it ever was, and he knows enough to listen his way into my space, to hear what happens in my office, who comes and who goes, and all I promise and do not promise. He is always there, there is no escaping him, and if I changed offices he would be there, too, or someone like him. He is there in the mornings when I arrive, he is still there in the evenings when I leave for the day. No doubt he lives in the city, he has squeezed his whole family into an apartment smaller than an office, he is not chasing by train the gentleman's dream of a country house that in this ungentlemanly age recedes further and further from us, as the city expands and the suburbs withdraw, until one can no longer reach one's house in the light, only in darkness, in darkness where there is nothing to see, the children are tired, too, they do not want to talk about their day even face to face, my wife, too, is like a stranger to me, maid of the house, we eat, watch a program, and then it is time to sleep, to sleep and to wake early if not refreshed for another day of the same. For he is there, he is always there, that is what distinguishes him. He does not commute between two worlds, perhaps for him these two worlds do not even exist, perhaps there is nothing to balance, everything goes out from him as from a single center, as noise does, and so of course the sounds of repair do not bother him, they are his repairs, as my sounds, too, are his now.

At lunch his family arrives: his wife brings coffee and sandwiches, the children carry their own chairs, two boys bear a folding table past my office; each day I see them file through the corridor of our office building like avatars of a lost world, content as ducks with their given order, and wait then for the other side of the wall to explode into laughter, crying or shouting, or the human sound of talk – sounds I am no longer used to on my side of the wall, sounds a man of my position simply cannot make: my children are at private school, they can not visit, my wife is in the suburbs, and when she comes to the city it is not to bring me sandwiches, I myself cannot bear the idea of having lunch at my desk – it contradicts everything for which I have worked, my image is not that of an immigrant with a paper bag in the center of a large noisy family. When I go out to lunch, my competitor remains at work, he is always at work, all that is gentlemanly concerns him not at all, even now he is no doubt on the other side listening to me, deciphering what I do even as I perform it, and if not my competitor then someone else, one of his family, while he himself even now while I complain to myself is running over the concrete, his hand outstretched, a contract in his hand, about to overtake one of my clients.

The New Laws

The old stone tablets still exist. The new laws, however, in our country are no longer written on such tablets, which are now blank, or rather defaced, but on scraps of paper, so great is the country's respect for the new, which can be changed at a moment's notice, for the people pride themselves on their adaptability, and the law is thought to reflect the will of the community – the people do not like to speak of the majority – which is always changing. The stone tablets are a reminder of another time. Out of reverence for tradition these stone tablets have been preserved, disfigured though they are, and less by time than by people, it is said, criminals or lawyers, for the difference between them is itself a matter of law and thus in the hands of the lawyers and therefore always changing, so that the scraps preserved between them might have the authority at least in appearance of the old code. So great is the people's reverence for tradition that strong men are employed only to shift the stones, so great is the people's love of the moment that messengers are kept only to bring in new scraps so that all trials can be conducted according to the latest ideas of the community. The immediate beneficiaries of this system are the lawyers, of course, who alone know the law on which it is said that the country is founded. Their power and wealth have increased accordingly, but so has the time necessary to study the law, itself out of date by the time it has been mastered. Thus, for all their love of the new, the interpreters of the law themselves recede necessarily further and further into the past, and no doubt as a rite of recognition as well as of humility it has become a custom in the trade to begin the morning by striking one's head against the stone.

This Will Be Yours

"This will be yours," the old man said.

The young man looked into the white rectangular space and saw that it had what he needed: a bed, a reading chair, and a desk to write on. There was also a wall that was only a window. "You have a very nice girl friend," the old man said. "She is not my girl friend," the young man replied. "But she is very nice." "And a very good friend," the old man said, "to find you a room." A dark bright look crossed the young man's eyes, and he smiled at the owner.

"You can use the kitchen whenever you want, in the morning, too, and don't bother about disturbing me," the old man went on. "I'm used to being disturbed," he added, gaily. He was a short old man, with a grey unhealthy face, and a bald red scalp which was disintegrating into transparent wafer-like white flakes. He spoke with a Polish accent, and this also pleased the young man, as if he had turned the city block back into his own ancestry and could now listen again to the alien sounds, frail as they were, of his own childhood.

"Thank you! Thank you very much," he said, and then shut the door, and looked out the window.

There was nothing in the window but the night. That was the way he liked it. At his last apartment there had been an office building opposite him and in the one before that a wall that had been white once but that had with time turned black. Now there was nothing but the darkness and the lights in the darkness. Even the noise of the city must be bearable at this height. Now only the uniform passage of traffic could be heard far below like a humming, nothing of individual sounds. At his last apartment he had had to rise every morning to the sound of construction, and it had been so impossible to listen to his thoughts in the noise that he had stopped thinking, or so he thought. He could see the river now, a sparkling absence flowing under the city lights, dark and dirty as it was in the day, and he imagined that he would be able to see the far hills in the morning, blue and furred like wolves as they moved west, and if he pressed his nose to the glass and looked to the right he could even see the bridge, its twin triangles of light shaped like the sails of a schooner, or the outline the sun leaves in summer on a woman's breasts.

"That is a good sign," he thought, as he folded his clothes onto the reading chair and thrust his body into the narrow bed. "A person who can think of woman, voyage and bridge together in light and darkness still has a future."

In the morning he unfolded his clothes, put them on again, and tip-toed into the living room. There were pictures of childhood and only of childhood on the tables, and there was a bed against each wall, instead of a couch or a chair, as if making it possible to collapse anywhere and at any moment. But each bed was empty, and when he opened the kitchen door he saw that the old man was there, asleep in the bed that had been placed between table and wall. Against the stove leaned a pink wooden leg. There was a hand hanging over the bed frame and on the old man's wrist he could see in blue the number that had been burnt into the flesh. How stupid he had been, he thought, how stupid and how selfish, and closed the door, and tip-toed back through the living room, past the photographs, into the room that was now his, and got back into bed.

A knocking disturbed him, and he went to the door. "You wanted to see me," the old man said. "I heard you at the door. Or you didn't want to see me." "I didn't want to disturb you," the young man said. "Not in the least," the old man replied. "Nothing can disturb me anymore." "I didn't want to wake you up." "Nothing can wake me up. I don't sleep anymore, I just lie there and wait for the light, and then I get up again. But you don't have to worry about disturbing me anymore," the old man added. "I'm going away. You're a lucky man! You don't know how lucky you are! You'll have the whole place to yourself, and you thought you would have only a single room! Lucky, lucky! More than you can know! I'm going away, for three months, perhaps more, the whole winter, to Florida, and no one will disturb you! You're going to be alone! You won't have to see me in the morning, when you make your coffee, or worry about me when you cook something late at night, or have a guest over." "I don't object to seeing you at all," the young man said. "Don't say that," the other replied. "It's no pleasure, for a young man – and I snore. I know." "Not at all," the young man protested. "Not at all!" "And I'm not charging you any more than for the room."

They came in the afternoon to take him away, the people of his generation, a man and a woman, each also with a number on the wrist.

In the window, through the polluted air, beyond the factories and refineries, the far blue hills could actually be seen.

The Empire of the Singers

or

A Desolate Place

For the song to be sung, and sung perpetually – for this is the goal, and only this, whatever is necessary – the day must be divided, for no one can sing all the time – alas! – no one can listen; and so when not singing in the empire of the singers, the singers do whatever is necessary to support the singing, not only of themselves but of the others, and thus the song is kept alive, even when someone dies, the song continues, so say the singers, at least those who speak, and so renowned has the song become that more and more singers have come to sing, more and more is necessary to support the singing in the silence that alone makes singing possible, and thus it becomes necessary for the singers to abandon everything and seek a desolate place where they can sing again in silence, a silence their singing necessarily destroys, renowned as it is, renowned as it must be, and thus no sooner arrived is it necessary again to abandon everything and search once more for a desolate place, and thus in time does the empire of the singers establish itself. Borders themselves are of little importance, song flies over them, words themselves can be translated. Of course, there are people who object to the singing, if not because of the song then because of the violation of the borders, not to mention the silence, a silence which they themselves no doubt want to shape in their own art and manner; and thus as the singers advance and the silence they need necessarily recedes, other people, opposed to the empire, start to attack even the signs of what the singers have abandoned. Thus in the name of the light since darkened the windows are broken, in the name of a future itself long past the stones are carried away. It has even been said that it is our right to destroy

the empire, as it is said that it is our right to build it again. And so the
singers continue to search for a desolate place, their structures abandoned even before they have been completed, and thus the empire continues to grow at the same time that it is destroyed and is known even
to this day as a desolate place.

The Statue

The statue shows two animals, each identical, one perched upon the other's back, mouth to its neck. Naturally, many interpretations have been written of this image, which still stands at the entrance to our city, on a site once occupied by a temple and later a church and now an office building. Even today when most people have ceased to care for written interpretations, outside of a few specialists whose work is said to be too specialized to be of interest to anyone else, people still speak of the statue. Even those opposed in their interpretations appear to find common ground: there are two animals, it is said, they are of the same size and indeed of the same form. The two animals are most commonly called lions, they have been carved with a realism that is astonishing, especially if one considers that there have never been lions in the region, and are thus to be read as symbols, it is said, and yet so worn down is the stone, so destructive has time been, that the features have been disfigured, and thus a number of resemblances have been noted, even to dogs, mounted one above the other, each identical. Whatever the beast designated, the identity of form remains; and it is this undeniable identity that paradoxically has produced the differences of interpretation for which the statue has itself become the symbol, whatever argument or interpretation one accepts. It is argued, for example, that the mounting beast symbolizes the triumph of the powerful over the powerless, a triumph which, it is said, will be reversed by the new age the statue was created to celebrate. Others see in the statue the actual arrival of that age: thus what is figured is the disfigurement of the old era, a traditional image, at least in former times; what we see are the powerless avenging themselves upon the powerful, although by assuming the role of the powerful it is said they are by their own logic preparing nothing less than their own demise and thus the statue celebrates the opposite of what it appears to celebrate. In either case, it is argued, a bestial struggle is taking place, one animal mounted on the other, mouth to its neck, and whatever the outcome or the meaning of such a struggle it has become a custom among us for our political leaders when we gather in front of the stone to acknowledge the mystery of our descent by speaking with one hand upon the beast.

The Order

The order has been established, and the rules of the order are known to all, if admitted by none, for this, too, is one of the rules. For we are known by our work, we members of the order, and this alone, and for this in particular we are criticized, at least by those outside the order, as if it were our order itself that was disordered, nothing less. True, there are those among us who do not read, who if pressed for a statement could only recite the company *credo*, such as it is, as if this alone were required. Yet there are also members among us who, if they no longer chain themselves to a rock, or climb the traditional column, still allow themselves to be walled up for their beliefs. The skill to launch a war has not been lost. Nor do we lack voices to bemoan the deformities we live among. Disfigured as the stones may be, we of the order still acknowledge our patron saint, half monk, half soldier, as he waits among us for the elevator, briefcase in hand, the great chimera of the century.

The Rules of The Order

The rules are read, not silently, but aloud, even if no one listens, for what was once the speech space in the order is now the rules room. It is in this chamber that the chapters are recited, together and alone, without books or even manuscripts, for members of the order are required to know the texts by heart, and thus the written word, if indestructible, is equally superfluous. It is in the rules room that the rulers themselves are buried; this is the ultimate honor and the final acknowledgment and proof of the ruler's importance, for the rules room is so renowned for the harmony of its proportions and the unity of its effect that it is said one has not lived if one has not seen it, so perfect is the space. At least such is the rumor. For to know the rules one must accept the rules, and in advance, and accept them forever, otherwise no entry is permitted to the room. One knows of its renown, if not its beauty – for over this no one inside has ever written, that is apparently one of the rules – only because of the complaints of those to whom it has been closed.

Saturn

Saturn sat down at his desk and looked at the white wall opposite him. He had worked too hard at the office recently, the days of leisure were far behind him now, he had actually come to like working at the office, tired as he was, and yet no one seemed to recognize the work for what it was, tired as they, too, must be. True, some people were aware of the old gods still, but this was of no importance at the office, even Saturn himself seemed no longer to take his own godhead seriously or to understand fully the purpose of his work. How could you have invented the office? people say to him, at least those who recognize him for what he is. Why? Saturn himself cannot understand this, cannot even grasp as he once did the tone of reproach, if reproach it really is, with which these words are expressed. Clearly, someone must have invented the office, since after all here it is, the place where we are today in our human history, divine as it may be, and nothing will come of nothing, but Saturn himself seems to prefer not to think of such things. He looks out of the window, one of the rewards he has received for his work, that gap in the concrete, and sees the city where the old chaos still reigns, out of which he once shaped the world, bathed in the underwater blue of aerial perspective like Atlantis drowned. Order and disorder, the office and the street: they are divided now, separated by a pane of glass, an invisible pane hermetically sealed. This absolute division still troubles the old god, whenever he remembers the days and nights of real creation, and troubled at his desk he lifts his pen among the white spaces and places on the page a word.

The Sign of a Civilized People

The sign of a civilized people is its art. That is what we tell ourselves, we members of the commission, and thus, by our own logic, we people are responsible, each and every one of us, for manufacturing the signs of civilization without which we could not even speak of civilization. We are thus aware of the importance of our work, doubt as outsiders may, for there are always outsiders – without outsiders how could we even speak of civilization? For today anyone can exhibit, anyone can present himself or herself as an artist: on the outskirts of our city there are places where no one is ever rejected; there the only outsiders are those who refuse to submit and thus refusing even to come forward cannot even be known as outsiders. But for the public places inside our city competitions are still held, approval is necessary, not the mere absence of rejection. It is this approval which appears to have occasioned recent rumors of a mistake, even of a joke, for how, it is argued, could we have placed as public art and thus as a sign of civilization itself a series of white boxes, each the size of an office, along the concrete walkway by the lake, each box identical, each box empty, each box with a single entrance no more than a gap in the material? Civilization? There is nothing inside, it is said, there is only an entrance into the dark, the dark which is always there, as long as the boxes are there, even in daylight, for this is what the boxes have enclosed, a dark that was not there before, a dark that is not even real, a dark which must therefore be considered the actual creation. People insist on this, those who have looked into the darkness, and more than looked, felt in the darkness, groped, on hands and knees, if necessary, and: indeed we in whose name the work has been commissioned have found it to be, as much as one can find in the darkness, a white space, darkly seen, admitted, nevertheless identical, within and without, in terms of the material, though inside, in the dark, who knows what one may find, if not now next time, if not next time later, and thus no one can say with certainty if all the boxes are alike, all the spaces identical, it is perfectly possible that there is something inside, whether intentional or unintentional is not the question, and that this is precisely what the artist in question is communicating, perhaps in opposition to the authorities, who no doubt do not want to commission works of art and are only fulfilling the requirements of their office. Who after all wants a white empty box? Yet if in opposition to ourselves, a possibility now under consideration, in spite of our work, these white boxes, should they oppose us, can on decree at once be removed and the original merciless light restored.

The Dwarf

The dwarf stands below my window. He speaks, and I listen; or, he speaks, and I try not to listen; but this, too, I cannot accomplish: there is the sound of a voice not to be avoided, but also not to be comprehended, a human voice, though the sounds, one wants to say, are not always human, but more like those of a troll below some bridge. He speaks to no one, that is the interesting thing. He carries on a discourse to which there is neither response nor listener, and this absence in which or to which he speaks seems to excite his voice to even more agitated assaults on the silence one feels might be there if only these attacks, more voluminous than ever, would cease so that one could hear whatever is there to be heard. But the dwarf will not stop, cannot be stopped, and that seems to be the one thing that his sounds assert, for the words cannot be said to matter, lost as they are in the noise of the city, and directed to no one. Freedom, family, work, and war: those are the themes, as far as one can make out, that concern the dwarf, those are the values in whose name he shakes the air I share with him, though the connection here is not all that clear, experienced as it generally is behind closed windows, and perhaps the lack of connection is exactly the point, the reason behind the incessant talking, if it is not contradictory to imagine a reason here, among such sounds as escape the erasure of everyday life in our city. No one listens, no one can listen, no one can be made to listen. And in this absence everything takes place, and must take place, as a violation of everything else. I for one have tried to speak with him, to make the word personal, and yet it is exactly the personal that is open to doubt, here, I am aware that I myself really do not wish to speak with him or to engage in intercourse with anyone unknown to me, on the contrary I wish him to stop speaking, if speaking is the word, to diminish the quantity of sound if not to increase the quality of statement, for the latter would cause me to listen, insofar as I wish to consider myself a listener, where quality is concerned, and I want to concentrate on other things in the silence in which I now realize I only can think. But even my request for silence must strike him as a noise, I can see that now, as an assault on the air in which he, too, must live, on the freedom which he can experience only by violating that of others, it seems, as I attack his even in speaking, though it is exactly this freedom we violate by speaking of it for which we must work and defend by war: so runs the dwarf argument, if I understand it, but understanding is precisely what cannot be presupposed, for there are gaps, necessary vacancies, and this is perhaps the consequence if not the cause itself of this dwarf talk: that no one listens. I myself have entered into the process, I have thrown open my window and thrust my head into the gap as into a guillotine to cry out: "If you must say something, at least say something worth hearing!" But this insistence of mine had the result of rendering me speechless. For what could I answer the raised fist below, what can anyone answer? What the neighbors think, or might think? What they talk of doing to this person they call a dwarf who has neither work nor family, only words, and who is not even really a dwarf? No, the fist is raised, the war invoked, the freedom simultaneously stated and denied, and I, too, am here for a purpose I do not understand, I, too, am a dwarf.

The Music

"I'm free to do whatever I want," the other said. Bohr went back to the apartment, for there was nothing else to do: it was four o'clock in the morning, at six he would have to leave, there was no chance of sleeping with the music, shared wall that they had, and if he complained through the wall the answer would be the same as that through the open door, chained as it was, "Whatever I want I'm free to do," even if the order was reversed. They were not of the same attitude toward music, clearly, nor toward the purposes of the night. If Bohr was not a sound person, that was no reason for the other to be silent, Bohr agreed. But if the other was a sound person, at least without light, Bohr was a sleeper. That was how it was with Bohr, no getting round it, when things got dark, he closed his eyes, and Bohr would be the first to admit it. And yet it seemed to Bohr that something shared had to be found, more than a wall, words through a chained door were not enough. If Bohr and his neighbor were not of the same race, that for Bohr was of no importance. Bohr could be white, Bohr could be black. But for the others things were reversed. Bohr was the other, thus for the other Bohr's request for silence was a statement of race. But Bohr was talking about music, music, and the night. The other could be black, the other could be white. What mattered was the music, what mattered was the night. It was four o'clock in the morning, at six he would have to leave. At six he would put on his own music, next to the wall, there was no chance of sleeping with the music-shared wall that they had, and if he complained through the wall the answer would be the same as that through the open door, chained as it was, "I'm free to do whatever I want," provided someone was there. But no one would be there, no one was there in the light. That was how it was with Bohr. There was only the music, the inevitable music, on the other side of the wall.

In the Distance

The protest signs could be seen from the office window, at least that was what people said, and I the fabulous office worker walked to the end of the corridor and looked out the window for himself. In the black street far below something white could be seen, it was true, something no larger than a piece of paper, though at the distance that separates office and street today what was written could no longer be read, if indeed anything was written, for it was always possible, at least in theory, that in an age of words the ultimate protest would be nothing but a blank, if protest there was. But this, too, could not be known with certainty. Of course, it was possible that this was exactly what the protesters wanted, if protesters there were, or could be, now, this calling into question of the simplest of things, at least at the office, if not especially at the office. At least that is what I thought. When I turned from the window back to the office, I saw what he always had seen: the desks in place, the corridors black as the city streets, the other people at their desks. "I have a head-ache," his secretary says, once I has returned to the end of the line, and in the tone he hears the sound if not of protest then of complaint. "If you're thinking of a personal day," he replies, surprised at the tone of his own voice, "they were abolished long ago. And as for a sick day, you have not been here long enough to qualify for one."

Tomorrow and Tomorrow

Macbeth sat down at his desk and looked at the wall. The bloody business was far behind him now, he had at last found a niche for himself, a place among people who shared his values where he was accordingly at home. The famous fears he had once entertained about old age and the loss of friends he had forgotten, everyone had forgotten; here at the office there were always people to talk to, if one person left another arrived, another had to arrive, empty space was simply not permitted, no more than doors were allowed to be closed; and as the old hero paced the open area where the secretaries were kept there was always a face that would look up from a machine to frown or to pronounce the once resounding name. No one remembered the unpleasantnesses of a former regime, at least not in public; no one believed in the witches; Macbeth himself had lost his interest in prophecy of any kind; he was now of high enough rank to be charitable, for the weird sisters there were hospitals today, a tenth of his income went to such causes; and if his wife was no longer with him something positive could be said of this, too: a man should stand alone, as should a woman, there is space enough for ambition today. Even in the most crowded of cities all you have to do to rise in the world is to enter the elevator, robed in the right gestures, and, as the doors close, look up and learn to wait.

Powers of the Realm

Coleridge once said that he had a smack of Hamlet in himself. No doubt the writer wished to bestow on himself a compliment; we do not normally make the same claim for our touch of King Lear or Macbeth, at least not in the same tone, although it may be equally true, and certainly not if we expect people to remain with us in the same room. And yet Gertrude had a different idea of the poor prince than did the romantic poet and critic; at the duel, turning to her husband and in front of everyone, she announced of her famous son: "He's fat and scant of breath." Of course, it is possible that this is what the aging Coleridge had in mind. And yet, despite Hamlet's mother, Hamlet has become an almost universally admired figure, this character who drove a woman mad, had his schoolmates murdered, and did the deed himself on his girlfriend's father. We at the office who know Hamlet often see him ghosting through the corridors, brooding in his black suit over the blank screen of a computer, and if there are no pirates today to set the hero free from the nightmare voyage this is nothing to regret, as far as we office workers are concerned, but rather a step forward, and not only in terms of verisimilitude, for what we want now is to keep the tragic at bay, it is the tragic we refuse to admit, the tragic we have banished from our spaces; here at the office, we are all on the same level, whatever our differences, real or imagined, here if anyone is a prince we are all princes, we powers of the realm, fat, and scant of breath.

Words, Words, Words

She knows what he is reading. She would know even if he had said nothing, just as everyone knows what the clouds look like. He is reading the words, words, and more words, words in which she finds herself, time and again. In the words she does not drown, she is not buried in unconsecrated ground, for in the words, there is no ground. All that will happen is that she will lose her father. She has this on the highest of authorities. O is for orphan, not Ophelia, and with a father like hers how can the curtain not fail to fall?

Mother and Daughter

"So you're going to – "

"How can you know that?"

"I read it."

"Where?"

"In your letter."

"What letter?"

"The one you threw out in the trash."

"You have no right to read what I write."

"Whatever you throw out becomes public property. Don't you know the law?"

"I know my rights."

"You have no rights – not in my house."

"It's not your house."

"Do you know what you are?"

"The doctor told you never to talk to me like that again!"

"Nobody tells me what to say."

"Don't you care about the consequences of what you do?"

"Yes – to myself!"

The daughter looked out the window at the flowering magnolia that had obliterated the rest of the view.

"If anyone's a whore in this family it's you."

"How can you say that – to your own mother?"

"You let yourself take money from a man!"

"What else should I have done?"

"Work."

"You think caring for you wasn't work?"

"You call that caring?"

"Then get yourself a job."

"Waste myself in an office – are you crazy?"

"Then get married!"
"I don't want to get married!"
"Then what do you want?"
"I want to be myself."
"And what's that?"
"A seagull."
"My daughter is not a seagull!"
"What am I then?"
"Can't you even remember?"
"You have no right to speak like that."
"I'm your mother – I can say what I want."
"Then I'm not going to listen."

She put her hands over her ears, but she could still see her mother's mouth opening and closing.

"I'll tell you something," the mother said, as the daughter began to sob. "As soon as you say what you are in this world, that's what you are not. As soon as you say what a person is like, that's the least thing she resembles."

Sick and Personal

A young woman falls behind in her typing. This is not her fault, we say, she is doing the best she can, but a woman with bandaged hands simply cannot type as quickly or as competently as a person with hands-free. The bandages are not her fault, either, we agree, for her hands were cut while she was trying to defend herself against a rapist on her way home from work. It would be better if she stayed at home until her hands heal and she can type again, we say, only to ourselves, but she is a new employee at our office and at our office you cannot stay home unless you take a sick day or a personal day and as a new employee she does not qualify for a sick or a personal day. She must come to work and type. Those are the rules. They apply to each and every one of us, equally, they must apply to each and every one of us, equally, so we are told. And so we watch her bang the keys with courage, but courage at the office is not enough, and each day the young woman falls further and further behind, each day there recedes further and further from her the promise of a world in which a day can be called personal, a day can be called sick.

The Enemy of the People

Grant sat in the train, the man in the black hat and peasant vest was only a compartment away from him, it was not necessary to make the arrest here, Grant himself could enjoy the ride. As an agent he considered himself of the old school, he did not like to make scenes; he and the criminal he had been assigned to follow could share unmolested the view in the window: the mountain ridges like the skeletons of prehistoric animals, the blank blue sky, the wildflowers that even now were saying hello and good-bye at once as the train wound its iron way through the landscape. It was all that Grant could do to remind himself of his purpose which at any rate would vanish as soon as fulfilled. At least there was nowhere for the other to go, he sat under his black circular hat bound with a floral ribbon humming peasant songs to himself as the factories and power plants rushed into the background. Everyone else on the train was dressed in modern clothing, and what this was Grant himself would not have been able to say had it not been for the traditional peasant costume, the black knickerbockers, white socks and shirt, the black vest and hat which, black as they were, were embroidered in designs at once abstract and floral, like the colors in the mountain rocks. When the train reached its destination the man to be arrested sprang up and Grant was right behind him, together they descended the steps to the concrete, the much taller Grant like the shadow at the end of the day. At this moment something bumped into Grant and he put out his hand to steady himself on the shoulder of the man in the *Tracht*, only now Grant saw that everyone on the concrete was dressed in the traditional black and white. Before him floated a whole armada of circular black hats, from every hand rose the smoke cloud of a pipe, from every mouth came the same humming he had taken or mistaken as a sign of the other. "You're under arrest," Grant said, to the being already slipping away from his hand into the crowd in which it seemed that one existence had been multiplied into the many. "You're under arrest," he repeated, if only to himself, "for crimes against humanity." And as he hurried, or tried to hurry, for this, too, was impossible, against the ever-increasing crowd, all of whom looked to his suddenly untrained eye alike, he realized that he must have come upon a festival of the old music, for gradually the humming about him increased until suddenly and at once everybody burst into song.

On the Rocks

Prometheus lay on the rocks, catching the last glimpses of the sun. Nobody paid any attention to him in the crowd, the eagle itself had long ago deserted the city, in the street that divided around the rock even the police did not bother the old fire-giver anymore, preoccupied as they were with the entertainers and thieves. Prometheus himself had lost interest in his sufferings, which without the eagle were less presentable, if no less intense, and preferred to regard the light in silence. No one spoke of his sufferings anymore, nor did Prometheus himself ever bring up the subject: no doubt it was assumed that it was the same for everyone and thus a subject of no particular concern to anyone, at least on a verbal level. Yet sometimes dazed by the late light, Prometheus recalls the days of his youth, when there was still something to rebel against if only his own story, and feels at once and in his liver the plunge of the old beak.

The Ancient Story

Orpheus went down into hell to have Eurydice released. Eurydice did not want to be rescued, Orpheus knew this, and this was the reason that he looked back as they walked toward the light: so that she would have the independence she had always wanted but which he like any other could not give without taking it away. It was this song that Orpheus sang, the song of separation, and not necessarily his own, or only his own, for which, redundantly, some say, he was torn to pieces, and by those who wished to preserve the ancient story.

The Myth of the Barbarians

The barbarians overthrow the civilized, so runs the myth, and proclaim themselves the civilized: there can be no real opposition to this, for those who might oppose the practice in the name of the civilized have been put to death, or silenced by other means, and those who raise their voices are termed barbarians and as such are denied access to all that is called civilized. It is said:

1) That the barbarians have no respect for individual human life and must therefore be deprived of their own.

2) That the barbarians have too much respect for individual human life and therefore endanger the community.

3) That both 1) and 2) are but half-truths, that this is essentially a power relationship, that to have power over it is necessary to have people under, and that therefore the undermining of the community, something of which the barbarians are accused, actually confirms its overwhelming structure.

In fact, in the absence of a meaning acceptable to all concerned it is said that these people have achieved a form in which meaning itself has been abolished.

This, too, so goes the myth, is part of the meaning.

The Unwritten Pages

The mouse people run into the space, imprinting the dirt with their claws. There is, of course, no such thing as the mouse people, this is only a way of speaking, and in fact it is no longer permitted to speak in this way. Space, yes, mouse, yes, for this is the model established in the schools by the masters, or mouse masters, as once they were known, compliant, docile, frightened, used to long hours of work and in closed spaces, inoffensive individually except in groups and then only against the individual vastly outnumbered. Mouse then, but not people, for people, or the people, even as words, might prove offensive, so argue the masters, or mouse masters, from their heights of learning, and thus the mouse people remains a forbidden if unavoidable term. But what do they do, these mouse people, or whoever they are, if not run into the space set aside for them, back and forth, out and in? It is said they have work to do, and in fact that is why no one knows anything of the mouse people, even the mouse people, if there can be said to be any such thing, for they are too busy working to discuss their work or the meaning of their work; in fact, discussing work among the mouse people is a sign that the speakers are not working and is thus grounds for dismissal, not only from the work place of the mouse people but from the mouse people themselves. Such dismissal naturally renders the dismissed incapable of representing the mouse people and thus no authoritative report exists of the mouse people, it is said, at least by the mouse people. True, outsiders have reported seeing the mouse people at work, but precisely because outsiders their reports are not to be believed, at least not among the mouse people, and in fact being outsiders they themselves are subject to instant dismissal, not only from their work but from the country, for as outsiders they clearly cannot have the same rights as insiders – that is logic, mouse logic, for you – not if the mouse distinctions are to be maintained; as outsiders the one right they can have is the right that makes them outsiders, the right to leave the country of the mouse people, exactly the right that the mouse people in their own country do not have and in fact cannot have without ceasing to be mouse people. No doubt it is this central absence where one would expect something like a right or rights that helps to explain the emotional attitude of the mouse people toward the non-mouse. Whatever the explanation, even in their smile – a smile for which the mouse people are famous all the world over, at least among outsiders – the mouse people bare their teeth, the same teeth with which even now it is said they are working their way through the libraries, consuming everything, destroying even the unwritten pages.

The Cave

The old philosopher sat down at his desk and looked out the window. The republic had long been a reality, no one remembered its inception, or the opposition it had faced or effaced. No other way of life was now thought possible in the republic. Even Plato himself had forgotten its origins or his role in them, honored though he was on official occasions, plumped out in his best suit and tie. The office which he occupied was a small space, though relatively large by official standards. Beyond the window, there were other windows, other offices, in which other people could be seen like himself at work in offices like his own. Plato liked the anonymity of office architecture. No one remembered what he had written, his own words had withdrawn their world from him, he, too, was now free of the classic struggle, it was no longer even possible to get the work published. Even Plato himself had forgotten the once famous parable of the cave and preferred to look out the window at the light, whenever it appeared, among the shadows of the office buildings. Sometimes the old philosopher would stroll the corridors admiring or attempting to admire the common things of office life. Sometimes when he looked at the black lines of the white ideal world he had helped bring into being he would recall fragments of what he had thought forever banished, the old words, the old song one can neither fully recover nor fully forget. Then other lines would appear on the ancient face; the characteristic smile would disintegrate; and on the lips – at least for those who could still read – formed something like the snarl of the trapped beast.

In the Old Part of the City

Jupiter found Prometheus where he had left him, bound to the rock, surrounded by other beings who indifferent to him were going about their business, strolling through what had become the old part of the city. The ancient thunderer did not recognize his former adversary, so much had come and gone, so many wars, intrigues and marriages, not to mention desk work. Prometheus himself had forgotten the words that had once come between them. No doubt this was part of the punishment, those who remembered said, for silence would be death to such a character. Others saw in the silence the only mercy possible. Prometheus himself no longer recognized the old tyrant, withdrawn as man's friend was into the pain which even as the years vanished continued to increase and which in fact like the rock and the eagle in time had grown inseparable from what he knew of life. As for the old thunderer, one of our senior citizens, pleased to be free of the office at last, he rhythmically beats his stick against the fixed and ancient stones.

The Cult of Judas

Judas was the true believer, and thus the kiss, according to the cult of Judas, for he believed, and he alone, in the story, and what he wanted was to show the others it was real. What happened afterward is known to all, if conveniently forgotten, for what could be more terrible, or more tragic, than that last forsaken cry? Judas did not cry, for he who had made the story possible had fulfilled his purpose and in silence could die.

Of this story three interpretations are said to exist:

1) Judas was himself betrayed, if not by the kiss, then by the cry.
2) There was no betrayal, only a commercial exchange, without which no story could take place.
3) It was Judas who performed the act of betrayal and who, through the betrayal, took on our sins; thus Judas is the one made in man's image, the one, in our time at least, worthy of belief.

What We Are

Priapus sat down on the park bench. It was lunch time, he was lucky to find a place for himself, for all the other deities had also been let out for an hour of light. The old wood god bent over, as if to scratch the cloven hoof, and head to the earth slanted a look up the skirts of the woman on the swing opposite. But that's nonsense, my companion said. Romantic nonsense! That's not Priapus, it's an office worker, and that's no swing but a park bench. Why must you make a myth of every-thing? Can't you ever take us for what we are?

At the Entrance to the City

The skin is removed with a dull knife, inch by inch, so that the outline of the cut in each and every perforation will be visible to all. The ceremony is performed in the open, and those who find no place, like those who stay at home or come too late, can watch the operation on a series of screens arranged for no purpose but this and with a commentary that leaves nothing to the imagination, for what we people can see with our own eyes we nevertheless like to have confirmed in words and images. Once the skin has been removed, and such is the surgeon's skill that it comes off in one slow piece, it is hung at the entrance to the city on a post which still bears the city's coat of arms and on which in former times the heads of enemies were deposited. This serves as a warning, it is said, though a warning of what is never explained, and in fact this openness is said to be part of the ceremony, for it is by such openness that we people the world over are known.

Absolute Symmetry

The office has been built according to the principle of absolute symmetry: for every opening to the left, there is one to the right.

The people in the office repeat its structure in their words:

"On the one hand," says A.

"But on the other," replies B.

C, who prides himself on seeing both sides of the question, remains necessarily silent.

A fourth person, unknown to the others, walks alone, noticing the odd angles formed by the intersections of interior and exterior space, the most unhappy and at the same time the happiest person in that place.

Heaven and Earth

"You care too much for civilization," my companion said, although not without difficulty, short of breath as he naturally was.

"Civilization?" I answered as the circular cinder track flew under our outstretched feet.

"You forget," he went on. "Heaven and earth shall pass away."

"Heaven and earth?" I repeated, for I could see nothing above the concrete but the advertisements.

"And the office?"

"Even the office," he said, with triumph, though not without regret, it seemed to me, as the cinders flew.

Picture Gallery

A man stands behind a woman, his hand on her breast, the rest of the room in darkness. In the next frame two women are embracing, their bare feet on something green, a young man plays the violin, nothing can be heard of the song, a boy sits with his head between his knees, nothing of his features visible, absorbed in the music no one can hear. You can see a ship, too, if you look, in the next space, crowded with figures, as if they were strokes of light, or of darkness, depending, there are other ships, too, crowded or not, ghost ships, unmanned, unwomaned, or with a single steersperson, dressed in black, black boats no one will enter who will return, church cupolas in the background, round as a mushroom, or a woman's breast, not what churches are meant to look like, steeples that have not escaped an Oriental influence, something of the minaret, something of the rocket, pointing toward heaven, a finger, an exclamation mark. In the next room the metaphors are all dead: the mother lies in bed, the children have drawn chairs up to the corpse, the husband is not there, the father, whatever one can call the absent man, other women walk in the adjoining room, candles are burning the wicks black, the cross on the wall has no body. The classical statuary comes as a relief, below them or above them. There are men, too, each one at a desk, as at an altar, each one alone, black briefcase set against the whitest wall. How can you tell that the woman in the darkness has to be Jewish, the breast touched by a hand that will never be yours, or that the music is really music, the voyage a voyage, the ships ships, and the woman mourned alive or dead, the statues real or the real statues? Apartments, offices, we have our galleries, our images, we tell ourselves, ourselves reflected in the glass we look through, and what we whisper as we look out is: if you can't get away, at least stay put.

The Horns of the Dilemma

"I want to offer you some work."

"It's about time something like that happened," I responded, turning my attention from the wall at which I had been staring for longer than I for one would wish to the visitor in the visitor's chair.

But as soon as I saw the pointed ears and the red cloth under the business suit I regretted the words; but it was too late – the office owned them.

"In advertising, I imagine," I added, grimly, for at the moment I could think of nothing worse.

But my visitor only shook his head.

"Public relations, then?"

This, too, apparently, was not worth mentioning.

"If not the private sector, then the government? Something for the Information Agency? Or the Department of Education? Unless it's one of the President's speech writers you intend to replace."

This, too, produced nothing.

I was at a loss for words myself, so I did what I inevitably do on such occasions, I kept quiet.

This must have been what was expected of me, for at last the Great Adversary said:

"It is very simple, here at the office. What I want you to do is to tell other people that I don't exist."

And on these words, he vanished.

I realized then that if I did as asked at the office, I would be forever lost; and yet, were I to do the opposite, I would be equally damned.

The Hunger Wall

The wall is built in the following manner: the poor are assembled and told that the wall is necessary for the nation's defense and that they therefore are contributing to the defense of the nation. The wall is to be built by hand and thus to have all the benefits of handicraft. The area decreed for the wall is a rocky one, in fact it is hard to imagine why a wall is necessary there, or why anyone would even think of invading such a territory, rocky as it is, but rocky as it is the rocks can be carried by hand or cart to the hill where the wall is to stand. At the end of each day food is distributed to the workers, but only when they are too tired to continue their work. Of course, the wall will never be finished. This is clear to all of us who have worked on the wall, by the time a new section has been reached the old section has already begun to disintegrate, rocks needed for the new must be transported to the old, rocks needed for the old must be transferred to the new, the longer the wall becomes the further we workers ourselves must be transported, and the further we workers are transported the less possible it becomes for any one of us to have a clear and distinct image of the wall. In fact, it is only because of our hunger that the wall exists, such as it is, and for this reason the wall is known as the hunger wall and to this day, it is said, serves as an instrument in the nation's defense.

The Herd People

The gods have withdrawn, the gods must be withdrawn, if the gods are to survive, that is what is heard today, among the herd people, yet there are traces still of the old presence, or presences, it is said, for without these traces it would not be possible even now to speak of their absence, or absences, and we people still speak, here and there, even among the herd we people still speak, and for this reason, it is said, the gods have withdrawn, leaving only the words, or word shells, names in which we still war, and in the name of the unnameable, it is said, to which some people among the herd reply that it is in the words that the traces reveal themselves, such as they are, and thus they wander through the cities, silently blackening the walls, writing unwanted signs upon the stones, or what remains of the stones, while others in the herd, and with an equal certainty, if equally opposed, as rapidly erase them.

The Pillar

The pillar shows a row of beasts of prey twisting round the column, as if woven out of the foliage from which they appear to rise, the leaves themselves still bearing traces of their geometric heritage, so that not only the leaves and traceries but also the animals themselves are symmetrically balanced even as the beasts devour each other, for there is no animal that eats that is not eaten in turn. This is all that remains of the old church. The pillar has been placed inside the new structure, an act not without opposition, for the message of the pillar, it is said, is hardly a consoling one, intricate as the art may be, if message there is, for this, too, is open to argument, and functionally at least the pillar supports nothing, it is only a reminder of an order that no longer exists and that for many would be better forgotten, and yet it is exactly this which others deny, insisting that in our time at least it is only destruction that is itself indestructible.

Declaration Day

The nation has been created by verbal act, it is said, its independence established by declaration. But what gives meaning to the verbal act, we people ask. The signatures of the participants, we answer. And what gives meaning to the signatures? The verbal act, the declaration. Thus the perfectly circular form of our argument, thus our respect for the circle as the symbol of perfection, and for this reason no doubt it has become a custom among us on Declaration Day for circular wreaths to be placed around the neck of each official speaker. Thus encircled, thus yoked, it is the speaker's role – a role consecrated by verbal act – to speak in circles to the people while, ring on ring – for this, too, is of equal importance – we people listen and applaud.

Department of Complaints

We have a new department at the office, the department of complaints, if not of protests, and as if by some inevitable logic this itself has become the object of complaints. Some people object even to the word, complaint, here at the office, some because complaints should have no place in the world of work, if not in human harmony, some because the space occupied by the complaint should be occupied not by the complaint but by the protest which, in a word, the complaint makes safe. Others complain that no complaint can under these circumstances be made real, or, if real, can be sustained, for the incorporation into the corporate structure of whatever opposition there is violates the opposition and thus displaces that which should remain outside inside and so is worse than nothing, for it amounts to an acquiesence to if not an acceptance of the structure in which the complaint can occur. That is the purpose, argue still others. To put it simply: make a genuine complaint and you lose your job. And what will you have accomplished then? No doubt all this has to do with the world outside, there are things that from time to time are simply in the air, and at the moment among such things are signs of protest. True, from our offices, high above the concrete, if not the earth, we office workers can no longer read what is written, that is a problem, of course, we cannot even be sure that the word is still written. What we see are only white flecks, floating in the air, we can only imagine the protest, if protest there is, as if our own white walls had been displaced outside, divided, and freely now could shift position, each sign carried by a personal bearer, inseparable from the person, bearing the chosen word. Of course, this may be only imagined, perhaps it is not a protest at all, or even a complaint, but something entirely different, we at the office have no way of knowing. Inside, at any rate, I know of no one who has ever made a complaint. I myself have often approached the office, out of curiosity, though never entered it, and have always found it empty, except of course for the person who must occupy it. And I am not alone. Many others approach, look in, and pass by. And perhaps this is as close as we can come to a complaint, or protest, in these white official spaces, we who ourselves are scripted on the walls.

Scham

Scham looked at the wall. After all these years, he was being passed by; what he had thought was his for a certainty was now to be another's; what for years he had considered his own department was being phased out; in the new restructuring even the labyrinth of walls he had come to call his own would vanish; the window itself would not survive. In the window that day Scham could see what he always saw in the window: other windows, other offices, other walls. Scham turned from the window back to the wall. From the other side came the sounds of the machines, writing and copying, and then silence, and then again the machines. This would be the last clear and distinct impression Scham would have of the office. What happened afterward every informed reader knows: Scham reached into the central drawer of his desk, removed the revolver kept there, then went out into the open area from which came the sounds. From the center of the open area, the policeman could see into each of the offices, for it was the policy in Scham's department – a policy that had nothing to do with Scham or any other individual – that the doors be kept open. Thus it was possible for Scham, standing in the center and steadily revolving, to empty the revolver, one bullet for each office. Then Scham put the gun into his interior suit jacket pocket, abandoned the open area for the elevator, made the customary descent, and went out into the darkening streets as he always did at the end of the day. There everything was as it always was, and it surprised Scham to see the people drifting across the concrete, as if nothing had happened, indifferent to his arrival among the shades.

Monument against Fascism

The monument against fascism has been erected in our city; it consists of an aluminum column, thirteen meters high and one meter thick, covered with a coat of lead, and placed over a shaft in the earth of precisely its size. Thus the absence below corresponds exactly to the presence above. People are invited to write their names on the column, the invitation itself has been written in a variety of languages, thus foreigners, too, may participate, and when the column has been covered with writing it will be lowered into the earth until nothing remains of the monument except a window for future generations. It is thus hoped that the monument will tell no one what to believe in, rather the people should tell the monument what they believe in, if anything today, even if it is only the worth of a person's name, a signature. Thus the monument against fascism. Only recently people have begun to deface the monument, people come in the night and scratch out the signatures, even the most despicable of signs have appeared. The authorities themselves have begun to criticize the monument, likening it to a modern tower of Babel, albeit ultimately inverted. Some object that this is not art; a victory column would be more appropriate, they say, if column it must be; while others for the money would prefer a few more meters of public transportation. Even those once most vocally in favor of the monument now argue for something different, something that cannot be desecrated or covered with filth, something behind bars or placed under glass. And yet there are others, and I am one of them, for whom it is this filth and desecration that make the monument the monument it is, for what is written, even now, shows us what we are, even if disfigured or defaced.

Marsyas

Marsyas hung from a tree, his withered skin a harp in the wind, some said, while others noted a resemblance to a melted clock in the desert sun. Occasionally a passer-by, mistaking him for a political prisoner, would inquire what had happened. But the victim was unable to answer.

In the silence the following explanations were supplied by the questioners themselves:

1) Marsyas had challenged one of the gods to a contest and lost, and this was the agreed-upon and in fact the traditional punishment.

2) There were no gods, Marsyas' challenge had of necessity gone unanswered, and to disguise the fact the authorities had placed the body where it was.

3) The challenge had been answered, Marsyas had won, and in despair had inflicted the punishment himself.

In the absence of any possible word from the victim, each of the statements finds its echoers, and in time the explanation of the story itself becomes a story.

A Slab of Bacon

"Justice!" cries the man in black, black and white, to be exact, and everyone nods en masse, as if they had understood, or else dozed off. The agent of revenge becomes its object and annihilates the play. Only Hamlet is silent. What is there to say? The ear is infected, the ear is always infected, the poison is working even now, in him, in everyone, like a silence, or worse, a word. "Treason! Treason!" voices cry, and at this moment it does not happen, what is supposed to happen, the story that Horatio himself is ready to relate. It does not happen, what is written, it cannot happen. Revenge tragedy is the tragedy of revenge, there will be no more tragedy. But we people love it, the hands applaud like mad, and at Christmas the authorities throw out a word, a slab of Bacon.

The Old Philosopher

Plato put his pencil down and looked at the wall. The poets were gone now, so were the musicians. Granted, when the elevator doors opened what there was of music could still be heard, the unforgettable lines he had thought banished would still rise singing among the papers on his desk. But even the old guardian no longer feared their effect at the office, the words floated like words among the other words before him. The old philosopher actually liked to stare at the wall, the white and empty space reminded him of a blank page, and this was the one consolation granted him, for he who had written the book was now condemned to live by it.

The Stealing of the Law

Among us it is a law that the law itself must be present, and physically present, when voted upon; no doubt this is part of our Roman heritage, this respect for the law, such as it is, and thus some of our lawmakers, in an apparently hopeless position, have seized upon the one sure means, itself permissible, if not of winning, for that in a hopeless position is clearly impossible, then at least of avoiding defeat: they have stolen the law, the actual script, and have hidden it somewhere among us, confident as they must be that no one will protest, knowing that while the law may protect others from ourselves and ourselves from others there is nothing that protects the law, and apparently convinced that no one will now say we must begin again, from nothing, with no script, searching among ourselves.

The End of a Myth

It was holiday time, once again, and, once again, exhausted from the interval between holidays, too exhausted, he told himself, once again, even to plan another holiday, the young man set off for the island which of late had become his place of preference, when not at the office, and, once there, once again felt his growing lack of pleasure in a place grown too crowded recently with people like himself, pleasure-seekers, exhausted from their work. At the tourist office, he decided to book a private hunting tour and the next day with the other tourists and the rented dogs set out on foot in what was left of the interior in search of the game. It was not long before they came upon the women in the grove. To see them in that state and situation was forbidden, he knew from the brochures, just as the forbidden was equally part of the program; and at any rate, he told himself, it was too late for him to turn back now: what had been seen could not be unseen. The women, as if aware of this logic and in fact the equal victims of it, did nothing to conceal themselves from his awkward and awakened eyes, but continued to enjoy what was left of the late light. Perhaps nothing would have happened, perhaps it would have been just one more holiday like any other, had not one of the women simply begun to speak. "You should not be surprised if, in coming here to destroy some beast, it is the beast that destroys you, for whatever we try to destroy comes back to destroy us, too." The young man began to argue with the woman, if only to point out the consequences of these words for herself, should they be true, but what he had taken as the beginning of communication appeared to be the end, at least what he heard sounded less and less like human language and more and more like the wordless barking of animals; but as he raised his own voice to fight against whatever this development might mean he realized that instead of forming the wished-for rhythms all that could be made out was the cry of a dying beast.

The Pit

X walked across the vacant lot to the pit's edge where a man in black and white, no doubt the supervisor, paper in hand, was directing the work in progress. "Excuse me," X said, but the man paid no attention to him, intent as he was on the work in hand. "Excuse me," X repeated, but again no one paid any attention to him, so furiously did the work proceed. The cross bars had already been dismantled, now only the vertical lines remained in place, like exclamation marks, they actually seemed to belong to the new work under construction, and no doubt it was this effect that the supervisor was now studying as he made his marks on paper which from X's point of view were no more readable than the scrawls of the winter trees already beginning to push forth their buds. Under the growing, almost imperceptible shade an outdoor restaurant had been established, the earth had already been buried under a sheet of black concrete, and from the ancient souvenir shops whose ownership had been transferred people were carrying away the last items left for sale. X pushed his feet forward and looked into the pit. "You mustn't do that," cried the supervisor, although by what right or rule X could not see, for nothing had been posted, and now even the exclamation marks had been removed and were being used to construct a fence that would perhaps one day enclose a play area. X could see bones there, in the blackness, if indeed they were bones and not roots, white roots, or stones. "Why can't I look?" asked X, and leaned even further forward, as he inevitably did when forbidden to look. Already the machines were covering what he had seen with dirt, no doubt on a signal from the supervisor, if supervisor he really was, the blackness was extending itself, the workers were advancing with their staves. "All I want is to look," X announced. But if anyone heard these words they had no effect, for already the earth was slipping away, even the little elevation on which he had thought to stand was vanishing, and the blackness was falling everywhere, over the stones, the roots, the bones, whatever the white things were.

The Place of Execution

At the time appointed for the end, the head falls. The sword is put away, the words as well, if sword or words there are, for almost no attention is now paid to the details of the ceremony. Even the epitaph has little appeal. It is said that this itself is a sign of the end. Before the cathedral there are other attractions, circus performers fight for attention, there are singers from different countries, musicians and magicians, and even beggars, not to mention the office workers competing for position. Under the circumstances it is difficult if not impossible to secure a place even to witness the execution, and as to the words it is no longer really possible to understand them, even to hear the words is a problem, it is even possible that nothing is said, that the people in question take advantage of these limitations if limitations they really are, merely to go through the gestures of speaking rather than really to speak, and only words no one would hear, no one would understand, words they themselves have not even written, and at any rate there are words enough already present, in the air, on the streets, even most of the people are dressed in words, single words, for the most part, no doubt messages, belovèd concepts. In fact, the authorities have begun to place the words in order, it is claimed, for if there are words, it is said, there must be sentences, order depends on this, and there must be order. Some insist that this itself is a sign of the end. Execution, right or wrong, only makes martyrs, we have enough dead, more than we can bear, and if in fact it fails to make martyrs this is even worse for a state such as ours, based on the law, as it is said to be, if that is what is said, hard as it is to make out the words. At any rate there is no place for the martyr today, the church doors, it is pointed out, have long been full. Stand with your head under your arm like a lantern and sing if stand or sing you must, even if the stone could speak no one would hear.

In the Blue

Neptune looked out at the underwater blue in which the city had been drowned. He was tired of the office. But he had not been given the transfer he had requested. He had no diploma, he was told, scholarly as he was, he was too old to learn new ways, and at any rate things went so well in his department that there was no reason to disturb success. Yet it was exactly this success that disturbed the old deity. Things went so well that no one realized the extent of his work, even if his work these days was confined to paper. Only in a catastrophe could he make his presence felt and then it was the catastrophe that the others remarked and even held against him. True, he still enjoyed a slip into the water, even at his age the vision of a sea-nymph in the blue was not unpleasant. But what he wanted now before he was ultimately retired was to feel the earth under his feet. He had even tried to argue at the office in favor of earth work, dangerous as it was, precisely because of his underwater world view he would be able to bring something new to the task. But the words of the god fell on deaf ears: if there were correspondences between this underwater world and the one above, no one expressed any interest in them, and old as the idea was something new was exactly what was not wanted. So Neptune is condemned to sit at his desk, looking out the window at the city submerged in the blue, waiting for the catastrophe that is bound to come.

The Last Boat

"The trees are dying," the young woman said, looking out the window. "Why do you say that?" the mother replied. "That's a cliché." "They look like gnarled hands, old women under earth, black fingers in the black, drowning." "They'll cut them down," the old woman replied, looking at her own hands, the ring like a smoke wreath. Behind the women came the sounds of the television. "That's all your generation does," the mother said. "Generation?" the daughter replied, looking at the absence of leaves, the far hill like a hull upside down, the concrete buildings barnacles. "Words," the mother said. "'Beautiful words. Why don't you ever comment on your father's work?" The daughter turned from the window to the bulletin board on which the work hung. "I'm going," she announced, looking at the images that accompanied the words. The father raised the volume of the television. "Where?" said the mother, raising her voice. "Where can you go?" "Away from here." "You will lose everything!" the mother cried out, for it was not easy to drown out the sounds of the television. "If you rebel, you will lose everything." "Don't be silly, Mother. There's nothing to rebel against." "'Words!" the mother cried out. "There are still words, words are important," she said, as if by repeating the words something might materialize. But whatever she said her daughter did not hear, she was no longer there, the words fell on the board and the board did not want them. Outside the concrete stretched into the distance, there were more words, wherever you looked words hung in the air, they rose from the concrete, they shone from building to building, it seemed the whole city in its words was burning. The young woman followed the concrete to the river that in the white night itself looked like concrete, a silence at her lips. Life, she said to herself, as a leaf fell, watching as the word turned. Love, I leap for the last boat.

Building the Cathedral

Today we are building the cathedral. For generations, we have been building the cathedral. For generations, it has been said that the cathedral will not be finished in our lifetime. This has been heard so often that no one really thinks any longer of completing the cathedral; indeed, this would be the worst fate that could befall us, we people say, for then there would be nothing for us to do, and the work of generations would come to an end. That this not happen we are now employed to destroy the cathedral, to undo the work of the past so that the future may build on us, according to the latest ideas, and thus, ultimately, a monument to a time outside of time incorporate all time into its building. At least that is what we are told, we humble stone carriers, we who have no other task than to shift the stones.

The Empire of Words

Sailing to Cythera

We are sailing to Cythera, says a voice over the microphone, no doubt the captain's voice, for it has the unmistakable air of authority, and another, somewhat smaller voice adds that for those of you who do not know what Cythera is it is the mystical island of love. There everything resembles you, there everything is calm, luxurious, and beautiful. But that is not what we are like, you say. That is not what we are at all. Let us out! We want to go somewhere else! But that is exactly where we are going, says the ticket-taker in a blunt yet scholarly voice. We are going somewhere else. You have simply misunderstood the instructions. It is not that we are *sailing* to Cythera, it is that we *are* sailing to Cythera, each and every one of us: voyage and destination, exile and homecoming, at once.

Masks

They were wearing their masks, Mother and Father, the Happy Family Masks, as usual when we came to dinner for the holidays. I looked at Beatrice and suddenly found her face, in comparison, vague, unstable, and exhausted. We were seated at the long dark mahogany table in the center of the otherwise empty room under the electrified chandelier. Father's voice reverberated behind his mask, as the manufacturer must have meant it to so that what emerged from the speech hole would have seemed a distortion had one not had time to grow used to such sounds. The mask had a stern look, even with the absence that constituted the smile, as if to say of the figure at the head of the table: I have come this far, I can go no further. This is the place to be. Mother's mask also darkened to an opening, though the designer had taken pains if not actual pleasure to intimate that this smile, far from severe, should be thought of as wistful and mysterious, reminiscent of sweet deeds done and suggestive of the good memories still to come. "And now for the *pièce de résistance*," said Father, sticking the king-size carving fork into the breast of the bird on the dark agonizing table. "A turkey," Mother added, no doubt assuming that an explanation was necessary for a woman who surely did not cook, and handed us across the polished lights the Happy Young Couple Masks they claimed they kept for us alone. "Now tell us your plans." I am not one of those characters who can claim to speak for another human being, it is more than enough to represent myself, so I let my Beatrice give voice to the career, the children and the houses to come, her voice already darker and deeper than my recollections of it, while I sat back at the long table, invisible to myself in its reflections, wondering how we were going to eat in decency with the masks we were wearing and doing what I could to find solace in the words.

Soap

I

Clean, he says, and she cleans, spilling the water over the marble slabs in the kitchen, sweeping the dirt away from the terra cotta tiles in corridor and living room, vacuuming whatever it is that dared to gather behind the television, dusting behind the *Playboy*s on the night table on her husband's side of the bed, even over the plastic bust of Socrates on guard above the magazines. She cleans and she cleans until clean becomes cleaner and cleaner the cleanest world a girl can grow up in. And their daughter grows up. She is a clean girl, cleaner than the others, say her parents, the cleanest on the block. Her father the image-maker turns to the agency that provides him with his models and so one day there she is, the girl next door, the one we envy, on our box of Ivory Soap.

II

One day Mr. Law, at a loss for images, takes his place in the interior darkness of what is known for some reason as an adult movie theatre that for reasons equally unknown has been placed in the building to the right of the office building in which he has his office. There are many of these so-called adult movie theatres placed for reasons equally unknown in the business district of the city. At the particular adult movie theatre in which he has taken his place there are only adults in the darkened interior, as far as he can see, but they are not only people from the business district, to judge by their clothing, as far as one can judge in the darkness of such an interior, an interior which as far as he can see only men inhabit, some suited, some not, some in shorts, others in long pants, and while he waits for the lights to dim completely he notes the presence and the absence of ties, the colors of faces and fabrics, before the darkness becomes as absolute as anything can be in such a place. The picture starts.

The picture starts. There is a white Colonial house, not unlike his own, in park-like surroundings, not unlike his own, and there is a stately door and behind the door there are three swings, not rooms, and on the middle swing there is a lovely naked woman who turns out to be his daughter doing unspeakable things to the man on the swing on either side. The image-maker closes his eyes and crowded with images gropes his way out of the interior darkness into the light of common day. He does not go back to the office.

He does not go back to the office but rather to Grand Central Station, arriving in time to catch the 3:21 and thus to let his black-walled tires crunch the white stone gravel in the family drive before his daughter has had time to go out. "How could you disgrace us like this?" he asks, only in a whisper, so his wife will not hear. "I have not disgraced you in any way," she replies. "I have given the world new images. That is what you do, Dad." "That is not what I do," her father replies. "I give them nothing. Nothing but incentives to buy. I enter their unconscious mind by creating links between their secret desires and material products and thus encourage them to imagine that acquisition can change their lives." "Then you have corrupted their minds and your talent solely through commercial considerations," she responds. "While what I give them, openly and with no secrecy whatsoever, are images of youth and beauty."

III

We read of her decline not in the local but the national papers: the soap company cancels its contract with her, the model agency abandons her, her new films fail to make money, she launches a singing career to no purpose and later appears at a publishing party commemorating *Hustler* magazine to sell off her clothes. The audience, expecting her to auction off the clothes that she is wearing, is disappointed to discover that she is putting up for sale only the odd items that she removes from a suitcase she has brought along for the occasion. People stop bidding. Not a few boo.

Then comes the descent into drugs. A child is born. The newspapers stop writing about her. The Laws sell their house. Instead of an image-maker, a constructor takes over. He paints the house yellow, no doubt to escape the meanings of whiteness now attached to the house. But yellow or not the house remains for us the Ivory Soapbox House. Even after he paints it blue.

Without the written word rumors thrive. Mr. Law is a broken man, some say, others speak, not without malice, it seems to me, of how excellent his golf game must have become now that he has given up his business and can do what he wants. Of Mrs. Law not a word. An old school friend announces that she has heard from someone who should know that our local celebrity has become a born-again Christian. She has a husband and a house of her own. Her daughter is rebelling against her. The rebellion will take the form of the clean life.

Wheel and Deal

I

You are there, when I come home, which makes me happy, which is unusual, not my being happy, I mean, when I come home after work, but your being there, when I come home after my work after you have come home after your work, that is what is unusual, after work, when I come home, that you are there. You look as you always look, after work, I tell myself. How else should you look? You look as you always look after work, you look tired, I tell you, and feel guilty myself, as if I were to blame for your fatigue even more than for my own, for not making enough money at my work to keep you from yours, when truth be told or what we once called truth it is your desire to work that sends you out to work, each day, each week, each year, or at least it did once, before you or I knew anything about work, when it all began, in such innocence. You look tired, I say, that is all that I say. I am wrong, of course. This time I am wrong. I should have said nothing. I should have waited for you to speak and not told you how you look or how you must feel. But something brings the words out, no doubt it is my own fatigue after work. You look tired, I say, no doubt meaning I do, for I have caught a glimpse of myself in the mirror over the fireplace mantle. You look tired, I say, looking at myself, and as I say this you move from the right to the left, from the left to the right in the mirror, on your way to the kitchen, I tell myself, and I am right, here you disappear, perhaps a meal is about to come out of that room, I tell myself, and only then do I realize that you are wearing nothing, your red soles, imprinted on my mind even now, draw me after them so that for a moment I forget to close the door behind me, which is unusual, not the door, a perfectly ordinary four-letter object, but my forgetting closure and consequently only hear and hardly the footsteps behind me. But having heard even if hardly I turn around and there he is: my surprise. My height, my age, perhaps a year or two older, clothes thrown over what seem to be his many arms to which in addition to the white T-shirt and the bluejeans there is balancing the boots in one hand attached at the end of the other a black and rectangular hard-edged briefcase, although I now realize in the liberty of almost infinite retrospection that the latter may also have been a saddle-bag, one of the implements of rescue or escape, for to my astonishment he appears to be wearing over his black locks a cowboy hat.

II

I go off on a long trip. It is not a business trip, for in my business there are no trips, and it may not really be that long, this journey, it only feels like a long trip, under the circumstances, without you, for I have decided to mark the distance that has come between us by extending it, I tell myself, drawing a blank between us, that is how you are to experience it, you will say, a blank space, like the space between words. That is what I think as I look up at the gray rose window of Amiens, for this far I have come, in my grief and guilt. Above me the kings are falling, they have been falling for centuries, these men, long before the revolution they began to fall. They are like the hours on a gigantic clock, and what they are doing is falling and rising and falling again. They are falling from left to right, from noon to six, from midnight to morning, and what they are wearing on their heads appears to be falling, too. They are rising to a fall, that is clear, they are falling to rise again, I say, not to you nor to myself but to the one beside me, the new one, under my arm now in an illusion of protection and warmth, for it is raining this Easter Sunday, a cold gray rain, and even the hot chocolate of the latest café goes only so far, I tell myself, though I will say it to you, too, later. They are rising to a fall, the kings are, they are falling to rise again, I tell myself, and this is where we are, now, on the other side of the window, outside, in the cold, after the revolution.

III

"But why the cowboy hat?" I ask, having returned from my *Wanderjahren* to what no doubt out of the force of habit I still call home, for in the inescapable liberty of almost limitless retrospection I am now convinced beyond a doubt that it was a cowboy hat I saw atop that head and not a motorcycle helmet or any other cephalic object. "How in this day and age and given the traditions of this country, such as they are, or were, could you even in a moment of wild abandon accept a man in a cowboy hat in what, foolish as I was, I once took to be something like our apartment?" "I must have confused the attributes of rescue with the actual thing," you answer, "and thus converted the latter into one more meaningless symbol." "I understand," I say, and walk to the window to remark in the rain on the concrete below us the resemblance between the circular lid of a garbage can and the rose window of Amiens seen from outside on a cold gray day. "I don't agree at all," you say, joining me behind the glass. "I have always thought that the garbage cans on our street look like the fluted columns of ruined temples," you reply, pointing out that like a family they have been chained together for their own safety, and from that moment on pledge yourself to eternal fidelity.

Rain

I

The music was beginning. There was no music. It was beginning to rain. It was not beginning. There was only the harp, outside, in the sunlight, on the white stones, in front of the double garage door, slid open to the dark, inside. Not to be played. Not now. Now that the music was beginning it was not to be played. Outside it was raining and beyond the rain it was not raining. Beyond the rain the sun was shining and the birds were singing when they were not. The vacuum was coming closer and above the vacuum there was the music. There were the double doors, closed now, a double cross, the shadow lines, wood on wood, white on white, only the light and not the dark inside. The vacuum was coming closer and closer with a music of its own. Inside the harp it was raining.

II

"Come in," thundered the voice, the voice on the other side of the door, and the other entered, obedient as the other was, a child, to the voice of the father. It was a strange room, with a strange bed, in a strange house, and there was the father, in the strange bed, in the strange room, the strange father in a strange house. There was a sheet over the father. There was a movement under the sheet over the father. Something was trying to come out from under the sheet over the father. "It is so good to have a week-end with you in the country." "Of course, it is good," said the father. "Everything here is for your own good." "But there's someone else," the child cried out, "under the sheet, trying to get out." "Of course, there's someone else," said the father, as the head of the woman emerged, above the sheet, in a scribble of hair. "There always is."

III

"Don't you see what is happening?" "Of course, I see what is happening," the father said. "A father always sees what is happening. The music is beginning." "The music is vanishing," the child said, "and I'm vanishing with it." "Of course, you're vanishing. It's only natural." He was now standing on the bed, in his long flowing African robes, as was his wont, the caftan like a fire on his head. "You mustn't be afraid. This is the normal course of life." "I only know that I am vanishing." Outside, the weather had turned. Inside. Something was contracting. In the rain. All that was left of the harp was the rain. Soon she herself would be the field.

Intimate Scenes on Video

"Look at me," the daughter said, turning the page. "Why should I look at you?" the mother replied. "All you do is read." "What else should I do here?" "Get married," the mother said. "That's what a good girl does."

The Indian walked through the living room. "What about him?" "What about whom, mother?" "The Indian." "Don't be absurd, mother. There are no Indians." "That is the tragedy," the mother replied, looking out the window. "Look what we did to them. And for what?" she added, staring at the new white picket fence that walled off the view. "Don't be ridiculous, mother," her daughter said, quietly, to comfort her. "You are the one in a desperate situation now, abandoned to yourself with nothing of your own."

"Then watch with me," the mother said. The daughter closed the book and sat down to watch with her mother. A girl began to play the piano in the wood. "It's the wrong video," the daughter said. "Father must have spliced everything together to economize. I'll run it fast forward." "No, I want to see how we were," the mother said. "I don't," said the daughter.

Where a face had been there was a splotch of light and then the room reflected in the screen. Then the blank vanished and there was the father. At first he looked as if he were reading or writing something, but then he lifted his hand and it was clear that he was putting together a puzzle. On the wall what looked like paintings were also puzzles lacquered to hold together.

The mother stood and took the vacuum from the closet, pushed the button and began to clean her way back to the sofa where she had been sitting.

The daughter rose, walked to the closet, took out a drum and began to bang it, slowly, in front of the screen. "What are you doing that for?" "It's part of the story," the daughter said. "Don't be absurd. What do you know about stories?" "More than you think," the daughter replied. "Listen." She banged the drum. "Can't you hear? Can't you see?" "Hear what? See what?" "The wood. The music. The music of the wood." "Nonsense." "The river. The music of the river." "Ridiculous." "The music of the river in the wood. And the Indian in the wood at the water." "Impossible." "And the sea, the music of the river in the wood as it opens to the sea, the music of the water as it blackens, even now, into light."

Vacuum Or No Vacuum

"You know what you are," the mother cried out. "You shouldn't tell me," the daughter replied. "You know what the doctors say." "This is my house," the mother answered. "I'm free to say what I want in it. And if you don't like what I have to say, you're free to leave." The daughter ran upstairs to her room. As soon as she had opened the door, she closed it, turning the key. Then she stepped over the objects on the floor and turned on the record player and began to sing. She knew that her mother would follow her up the stairs as if drawn by a vacuum, and that even now her mother was shouting at her to clean her space. But it was her room, vacuum or no vacuum, she could do what she wanted here, and she knew that the singing annoyed her mother, for the sounds on the other side of the wall grew louder, they always grew louder, whenever she sang. She could almost make out the words of her mother, even above the music, although she knew what there was to be said and not to be said, the sounds did not need to articulate themselves, whatever they were, she could outsing them. Then the vacuum came. She stopped singing and cried. Then she sat down at her writing desk and put on make-up. It was silent now, she turned off the music, then she went downstairs. Her mother was sitting at the round table in the dining room, it was much smaller than the rooms she still remembered from childhood, the night in the window, so that the whole room, brightly lit as it was, hung in the darkness. "I've known tragedy," the older woman said, as soon as the other had entered. "And I've known comedy." "You've had a full life, mother," the daughter agreed, sitting down opposite the other and looking at her image in the dark glass. "You've experienced everything." "That's true," the mother sighed. A man's head appeared in the window behind the images. The man was moving through the bushes in the darkness. They could hear the sounds. "He looks like your father," the mother said, not bothering to

look. "That's the secret with these older men. But what I don't understand is why at his age he still has to move through the bushes in the
darkness." "He's afraid," the daughter answered. "He's afraid of you. He
thinks you don't like him." "At least your father always had a job," the
older woman said, turning from the window to the wall as the daughter, too, abandoned her. "I don't know why you're hurrying," she cried
out. "It does not matter. When we are here, they are there. When they
are here, they are already leaving."

Life Is a Cabaret

1

"So this is where you are now."

He turned away from the white wall and kissed the cheek presented to him.

"Didn't you hear us speaking on the other side?"

"I did hear voices."

"Then why didn't you answer?"

"I thought it was only my sister, speaking to herself. She sounds very much like you."

"There is a resemblance," his aunt admitted, looking at the wall.

2

"This is a new chapter in your life!"

The young man scraped the paint away.

Where the paint had been, in flecks, like ashes, the wood showed through.

A ladder leaned against the house, its shadow on the white already painted. From the ladder, on a hook, a small tin could be seen.

3

"They're kicking me out!"

"How can I help?"

"Let her stay with you."

"Out of my life!"

"That's impossible."

"The house must be sold."

"Into the street!"
"Can't you rent it?"
"The bank's foreclosing."
"Like a whore!"

4

"I know you loved your mother, and at this moment it's only natural if you feel pity."
The young man continued scraping.
"But you have to remember that people get exactly what they deserve in this life."
"Poverty! Absolute poverty!"
"Do you mean death?"
"And the madhouse!"
"She has no sense of reality, does she?"
"On the contrary," the young man replied, and went on scraping.

5

"You don't understand."
More and more of the original wood was showing through.
"There is no grief."
"I'm an actress!"
"There is no death."
"A seagull!"
"What is there, then?"
"Don't you understand?"
"Love!"
"A seagull!"
He scraped a streak of paint off of the wall.

6

"Life is a cabaret!"

The young woman began a cake walk in the shadow of the mulberry bush, her fingers catching at the sun, a parasol's stays.

"Life is not a cabaret," the older woman said, sternly. "Life is a school."

The younger woman began to sing.

"A school from which everyone graduates."

"Life-is-a-cabaret!"

"Don't you at least know the rest of the words?"

"Life is – "

Another layer fell from the wall.

7

"The words are important."

"A cabaret!"

"You can say what you want."

"Life – "

"But some words are more important than others."

"Money!"

"Love!"

"Liza Minelli!"

"For example."

Back and forth went the scraper.

8

The surface of the wood could now be seen, the long grains clear as birds.

Silently, in the shadow of the mulberry bush, the two women embraced.

Then, the older woman began to show her niece how to perform a proper cake walk.

Beyond the strutting figures the new shopping center could be seen: the cinder blocks of its rectilinear structure had not yet received their colonial facade.

9

"You should now think about your father."
"He left us," the young woman cried out. "That's all he ever did!"
"He deserves at least a call."
"Absolutely penniless!"
"Out of respect."
"For nothing!"
"You should respect your parents."
"Sex! Nothing but sex!"
"As an act of love."
"Poverty and death!"
The white was gone; the young man turned the corner, and went on scraping.

10

"Life is a cabaret!"
"You don't understand."
"A cabaret!"
"That is an ironical statement."
"Life – "
"It is not serious!"
The younger woman paid no attention to the words of the older critical woman; she went on singing.

11

"What about your father?"
The young man continued scraping.
"Are you going to see him?"
There were no birds now.
"Or are you going to wait until he, too, is dead before you do anything?"
More and more paint fell from the house.

12

"I must go."

She kissed each person on the cheek again, then opened the car door. Inside, she thrust her head back over the half-raised blade of glass and waved at them.

"A family visit, the old values, hard work!"

The older woman smiled, turned to her image in the mirror, grimaced, waved again, and disappeared.

"She's getting divorced," his sister said. "You should feel sorry for her."

Turning toward the house, she added:

"And she could have been a good actress, too!"

A moment later the voice of Liza Minnelli could be heard singing from the open window.

The Blicks

"What a surprise!" said Mrs. Blick, opening the back door and looking into the darkness. "And you're here, too!" she added. "Either my eyes are going bad, or he's really blotted you out!" Young Blick put down his briefcase on the welcome mat and embraced his mother while the other woman watched in shadow from the flagstones. "But what's happened to your guitar?" his mother cried out, suddenly, only now noticing the twisted shape on her son's back. "A police car ran over it." "A police car?" Mrs. Blick said, looking intently at the other woman in the darkness, as if whatever had happened must have been her fault. "I do not want to hear a story about my son and the police!" "But nothing happened, Mother. We were only hitch-hiking," the young man said, trying to console her. "Except to the guitar, of course." "It looks like one of those early paintings by Picasso," Mrs. Blick observed, and closed the door. In the living room young Blick saw his three sisters sitting on the sofa looking out the window at the night. The three girls were all dressed alike, as was the custom in the Blick household, wearing pink pinafores with blue bows round their waists as well as in their hair. They all jumped up at once when they saw their brother, ran across the room and threw their arms around him, so that he could hardly extricate himself from one girl before another was hanging round his neck. Then they saw the stranger looking at them and straightened up, each extending a little hand for the woman to shake. "She doesn't say much," his mother whispered, behind the other woman's back. "She doesn't say much," her son replied, "but she sees everything." The Blick house was a modern split-level and young Blick climbed the familiar steps to the passage where the bedrooms were, pushing open the door to his old room with his foot, his guitar on his back, his briefcase in his hand, and his fiancée behind him. Once the two young people were in the room, he closed the door with his free hand, put the guitar on the desk, set the briefcase on the narrow bed against the wall, clicked it open and one by one began to remove from within his fiancée's clothes while she undressed. "You're better looking than I thought you'd be," said Mrs. Blick, as soon as she had opened the door, which like all the doors in the Blick house had no locks, and entered the room. "My son's a lucky man!" Then came the soft approaching sounds of his sisters followed by the crunch of gravel in the driveway. "Who could that be?" young Blick asked, for no one visited the Blicks so late at night. "It's your father," his mother replied. "I told him you were coming." "But we aren't speaking to each other. And you know that he does not approve of me bringing a woman home." "Things change," his mother reminded him. "Things always change." "We can leave by the window," said the young woman, climbing onto the desk. "Do you mind if I help," Blick asked, lifting with one hand the blade of the window while with the other he stuffed her clothes back into the briefcase. "Now you see how it is," he added, tenderly, before she jumped. "Life here is impossible and we love each other."

Parent and Child

I

"You have no rights."

"I'm not talking about rights."

"What are you talking about then?"

"The absence of rights."

There was a pause before the voice went on. "I'm talking about love, about the other as other, in other words, and anyone who takes away what he or she calls rights has lied to put them there in the first place. That is the danger today, not a fascist government but a fascist society, of people who claim to take away the rights of others they have secretly and surreptitiously bestowed."

II

The police burst into the room at six-thirty in the morning, when the two lovers were still asleep. Or perhaps they did not burst into the room, perhaps they even knocked on the door, there being no buzzer, and waited patiently if not politely, one smoking a cigarette, against official regulations, which he put out as soon as the door opened, or a moment before, crushing it under his heel not with the usual sidewise motion but rather with a simple back and forth sliding of the boot, forwards and backwards, backwards and forwards, the cigarette under the sole flattening, a black ash stain on sole and carpet, and then they were in the room, pushing the young man aside, fingers to chest, nothing more was necessary, sending him flying over the orange crate that served as bookcase and tabletop, with the result that the crate itself tipped over, in spite of the two books weighting it, Chaucer and Shakespeare, the complete works, spilling the little Cézanne still life off of the scrap of Persian carpet covering the crate – a ceramic bowl, three apples, an orange, half a pear and a knife, the bowl shattering on the floor, the apples, orange and pear bouncing off his feet and rolling onto the wooden floor, the knife clattering – and the next thing he knew two guns were drawn and he was looking up one of two deadly black holes.

The other gun was pointing at her, still in bed. She must not have been awake when they entered, hard as that was to believe, and now incredulous she had drawn the sheet up to her neck and was staring in horror at the pistol pointed at her mouth. "There must be something here. Let's have a look," the other said, and the other, the other other, took hold of the sheet next to her foot, she pulled from the other side, and then he let go, sending the object in question flying over her face.

III

Mr. and Mrs. Parent came to town. They visited their daughter in her flat. Mrs. Parent was very proud of her daughter, she told her husband of thirty years as they stood outside in the city snow. It was a major accomplishment for a woman to have a place of her own. "Time will tell," Mr. Parent said. "Time will tell." Inside the apartment, Mrs. Parent hugged her Baby and then began to open all the doors. "What are you looking for, Mother?" asked Baby Parent. "I'm looking for the other room," Mrs. Parent announced, with the sense of purposiveness for which she was known. "There is no other room," Baby answered. "It's not a tragedy only to have a room of your own," Mr. Parent said. "Nonsense," said Mrs. Parent, once again refusing to believe what other people said. "There is always another room."

But there was no other room in the apartment. "At least there's a bathroom," said Mr. Parent. "Look on the bright side." But Mrs. Parent was looking at the new bed that she had discovered through the process of elimination must be her daughter's bed. "A double bed?" said Mrs. Parent. "Why does a single person need a double bed?" "I am a restless sleeper," said Baby. "Then there's something wrong with your life," answered the mother, sat down on the bed, and began to cry.

IV

When Child came in to say good-night to his mother, he found
her where he had left her after dinner, in front of the television, a drink
in her frail right hand. "I've come to wish you good-night," Child said.
"What a good child," she answered, rising. She took his head in her
hands by the ears and looked at him a long time, as if trying to convince
herself that in spite of everything he was real. Then, tightening her
grip, she began to bump his head against the wall. Child smiled at his
mother. "You can't forget me that easily," he said. He had a lovely smile,
Child did, people often told him that. "Go ahead, mother," Child said.
"I'm not at all angry. One somehow does not get angry at one's mother."
Child's mother seemed not to hear, or if she heard not to acknowledge
what she had heard. She went on bumping the head against the wall
while Child kept on smiling, his eyes focused on the advertisements
floating across the television screen. "Thank you, son. It does me
good," Mrs. Child said, "to let out my feelings in a way that has no
real consequences." "I perfectly agree," said Child. "Now that Father
has left you it's only normal not to say natural for you to take part in
a substitution chain, absurd as the individual links may be." "I'm glad
you think that way, Child. It shows a great deal of maturity on your part
and thus reflects well on the values and upbringing that at great cost to
ourselves your father and I have given you." "I couldn't have expressed
things more sublimely myself," said Child, as once more Mrs. Child
smashed the head against the wall.

V

Child decided to take a job at the office and it was not long before
people began to speak of him as someone with a future. Perhaps it was
his capacity for obedience, for repetition, and for silence, if not for
certain words at certain times, or certain silences at other times, even
sounds, sounds and silences, parsed and parcelled among the other
sounds and silences. It was not long before Child had a desk of his own,
then an office, a number, a name, a secretary, and soon the women were

swarming over him, a person with a future, a future parent himself; and then one day, for reasons Child himself did not fully understand – a chance remark, or the absence of one, a misplaced solidarity, the intimation of a moral principle where obedience or repetition might have been more of the order of the day, or obedience or repetition where the intimation of a moral principle might have been more in order – Child found himself without an office, a number, a name, on the other side of the office glass.

VI

"You have no rights," Baby said to him. "You don't play the game, the game plays you." "I'm not talking about rights." "What are you talking about, then?" "Love," Child said. "Love and responsibility." Baby laughed. Or perhaps it was Child, Child first, and then Baby. Or Baby first and then Child. One or the other. Both, perhaps, separately. Or together. One or the other. Both, then. "Love and responsibility." "What do you mean?" "The dignity of the human being before God and the absence of God, equally."

VII

"I see," Baby said. She decided to get a job. After pondering long the essential as well as the existential differences between being a waitress and a secretary she opted for becoming a topless dancer, passing the job qualifications interview with flamboyant ease, then climbed onto the pedestal that would be hers every night until it was not. Child stayed at home and did the household work, for which it turned out he had an incredible absence of talent, while Baby thrilled the male multitudes with her art, such as it was. Child was proud of her, even from a distance. She had liberated herself. As to himself, a potential orphan, Child did not know if he should bemoan his fate or celebrate it, mistaken once again that the choice was his.

Manpower

I

It was going to be the games today, the games and drinks. That was what Manpower had in mind. As a college graduate, the clerk announced, he was lucky: he was going to have the first pick of jobs. The other parked the vehicle, together they took down the Coke machine and with the dolly wheeled it into the light and then out of the light into the building. He was surprised to see the women sitting in a row, inside, many in headscarves, bent to their machines, for after all this was apparently an elegant suburb. "If you're going to feel sorry for them," the other said, "slaving away in the darkness, then think of how I have to work, too." By the time the sentence was over they had wheeled the Coke machine into what looked like a concrete cube. Only when the other pressed a button did he realize that they were in an elevator. "Watch out!" the other cried out, suddenly, but when he looked he saw nothing to watch out for except the women slowly slanting away from him. Only when the women had vanished did he realize that this particular elevator did not close from the sides but from above and below, withdrawing his arm too late while the doors like huge jaws snapped shut.

II

"There has been an accident," he said, into the black receiver of the public telephone at the hospital. "I have been hurt, but nothing has been broken." There was a pause, a little black scream of a pause, and then the voice of his wife began to grow in strength. "It is the wrong order," she said. "Absolutely the wrong order. You should have started at the end and said that nothing had been broken and only then added that you had been hurt. Then I would not have had to imagine the worst."

III

"Think of this as yours," said the writer, showing him the desk, the telephone, the pad of paper and the pencil. "I have a special line, everything here is paid for in advance, so you can call anyone you want anywhere." The writer it turned out was working on a study of new forms of communication and it was to be the job of the young man, as a college graduate with a temporary liability, to conduct interviews by telephone. At the end of his work he called his wife. "If you're calling me to ask me to help look after you, now that you've been hurt," she said, "I want you to know that I consider your pain a form of illness and that illness makes me ill and that no husband has a right to make his wife ill." "I'm not calling as a husband," the husband said. "What then?" the wife asked. "As a person." "A person!" she cried out, and began to laugh. "A person's an abstraction. Don't you know there's no such thing?"

A Hell of a Story

I

"Look at this graph," Satan said, spreading something like the sky on the desk.

"Here are the buildings – "

"Excuse me, but everything's flat."

"Of course, everything's flat. You've lost a dimension."

"Don't be ridiculous."

"You're the one who's being ridiculous. Do you think love has no dimension?"

He pointed at the piece of paper on the desk and began to speak of the profit and the loss.

II

At lunch break there he was again, sitting on the park bench provided in the city for such characters by the government absolutely free of charge.

"I don't know why you keep calling me Satan," he said. "I'm only another character who works at the office, just like yourself." "Denial of your existence," the other replied, "only confirms it." "I suppose you think this is hell, then," Satan said, looking at the smoke rising from the manhole cover in the middle of the street. On the far wall someone had scrawled in large black letters:

THERE IS NO CERTAINTY

Someone else had added, equally in black, but in a much smaller script:

Are you sure?

"Only you're absolutely wrong, I assure you," Satan added. "It's only a place, like any other." "You can't fool me," the other replied. "I know that denial is the ultimate form of admission and that where we are being predicated on where we are not is riddled with absence as the very condition of being." "Actually, I wasn't thinking of that at all," Satan said. "I was observing the wonderful diversity of people in the city. You speak as if there were only one or possibly two models for behavior. You haven't discovered the age of the individual yet." In the street other people were hurrying back to their offices. "The age of the individual – ", the other began. "When I was your age," Satan went on, paying absolutely no attention to what the other was saying, "I, too, suffered from the torments of love. Where I was, she was, especially when she was not there, and where she was, I was, especially when I was not, the presence of absence became a figure for the absence of presence until, finally, there was nothing to do but admit what was happening and break things off.

"But now I really must get back to the office," he added, and faded on the sounding of a horn.

III

At the office there was nothing to do. He had worked hard recently, hard and efficiently, so hard and so efficiently that he had literally stopped the work machine, and so on entering the office he did what there remained to do, he opened the door to the small white windowless space that was and would be considered his until it no longer was, closed the door he had just opened, removed the so-called sport jacket males in his position were expected to wear, placed the object in question on the plastic triangle provided by the production manager for precisely such a thing, swung the door open once again (a closed door being out of the question), walked to the far side of the black executive desk ordered by the production manager for just such an executive, sat down in the matching black executive swivel chair, and then lifted his eyes to the view he had created simply by opening the door.

IV

Satan was sitting on the park bench once again, his right leg crossed over his left, writing down something in a notebook.

"Love and chaos, order and disorder," he said, as the other sat down. "Binary oppositions. What do you expect? They always collapse, each into the other.

"What makes you angry, of course," he added, directing his attention to no one in particular, "is the fact that you have become a number in a series without end."

"When I want your opinion, I'll ask for it."

"No, you won't," Satan replied. "I have to make myself felt now. It was easier in the old days, you know, before the Age of Democratic Egotism and the Dissolution of the Self. Then people were afraid of me, if you can imagine such a situation. Now just look at them all moving about like molecules – collisions, attractions and repulsions, dispersals and further dispersals – and you'll get the sense of order we have to work with today. Not to mention the American Dream. That was the supreme invention. Exploit your neighbor like yourself, disown the past for the present and the present for the future, and whatever you achieve consider it worthless in the light of the promise to come. Absolute self-destruction," he said, not without a tender smile, "not to mention the annihilation of all values. There is nothing like the pursuit of happiness to guarantee the opposite. I'm describing your childhood, I hope you understand, the dinner table talk, and the role of power in family relationships.

"And don't tell me that I don't exist. That's the beauty of the whole structure, or what's left of it. For as soon as you think I don't I do."

V

On both sides of the street, the office buildings rose like the two sides of a book. "Everything here is text," the writer noted, "even what isn't," and shielding the notebook with one hand so that no one could see what was written added a word, then thought better of it and crossed it out. Let someone else pick up the story, the writer concluded, as the sun left the street in shadow and, with a click, snapped the book shut.

Art Work

"You're late."

"We've been making art."

"That's no excuse for being late."

"You call what you do making art?"

"I don't care what you call it – it's what we do."

"Lying naked in a field in a huge crowd – like pencils in a box."

"You don't put pencils in a box in a field."

"You don't put naked people in a field."

"That's the point."

"And then what do you do with them?"

"You photograph them," the father said, "and sell the photographs."

"And you call that art?"

"I don't call it anything."

"And what do you get out of it?"

"A cold," her father answered.

"The true work of art is the video," the daughter explained. "But he sells the individual stills to pay for it."

"A video of people who aren't even moving – that's the end."

"The end of what?"

"Civilization!"

"As you know it," the daughter said. "That's what we're working for.

"And you'd be surprised how much movement there is," she went on. "People can't keep still. Even a cough changes everything."

"I won't have my daughter lying naked in a field with hundreds of other people!"

The mother began to cry.

"You don't understand, mother," the daughter said, gently. "You simply don't understand. There are no borders, now. It's off the walls. It's not even inside anymore."

"Of course, I understand," the mother answered through her tears. "Why do you think I'm crying?"

"You think he'll betray me, mother, as you've been betrayed. That's why you're crying. Don't think I don't know. But it won't happen like that.

"If there's to be any betraying around here," she added, not without pride, even if only in a whisper, and not to her mother alone, "then I'm the one who's going to do it!"

This Week in Paris

1

I can see the advertisement on the wall inside the subway: a young man with his fist raised, a look of triumph on his face as if he had just clinched a fantastic deal, and over that clenched fist the words: "I speak Wall Street Business English." It is the word Business that is new. Wall Street is no longer enough, apparently. Things have changed since my last business trip. Wall Street has lost if not its aura then at least some of its singular function. I notice that I am the only person in a business suit inside the car. I am also the only person looking at the writing on the wall.

2

In the new film, "Sex: The Annabel Chong Story", Annabel Chong, born Grace Quek, twenty-two years of age, the daughter of a Singapore family, breaks a world record. Her "gang bang" – 251 men in 10 hours – recorded live on video, has made her a star of the pornographic world. Fascinated by her experience, the American documentary director Geogh Lewis sets out in quest of the story behind the story.

3

It is too hot inside, I think, it is too cold. That must be why the window has been opened. Outside a man is reaching inside for a woman's purse. It is a monumental purse. A woman with a baby carriage is distracting the woman with the purse. Perhaps the three of them are in this thing together: the man, the woman, and the baby. The purse can not get through the opening, not at that angle, not with that monumental form. The lights go off. When the lights come on, the mother and the baby have vanished. The man, too. There is no purse, there is no trace of the purse. When the doors open, it is another world.

S/he

I

The avenue rose into the blue as if it were going straight to heaven; but this was only an illusion, of course, and once you had made your way to the top you had to start down again.

The apartment was small, the size of an office, perhaps smaller if the office were large, and the bed was the size and shape of a desk, pushed against the wall, and against the opposite wall there was a table, equally rectangular, which served as a desk, except for meal times, its surface covered with a city of books, and beyond the table there was a window in which the books became a city.

Then the clouds came and everything changed. The rain came down in slanting lines, the sun came out for a moment and then the lines were like the strings of a harp shining in the light. Then there was no light, there was only the rain, in prison bars, and the remembered rain was beautiful and ugly at once and then there was no rain and it was ugly and beautiful that there was no rain. The prison bars vanished, so did the harp strings. A person sighed, put down the pen, looked at the wall and thought of the blue, frozen light of diminishing glaciers.

II

"Your eyes look worried."
"Your eyes look searching."
"What are you worried about?"
"What are you searching for?"
"The reason for your worries."
Had it gone like that, the scene? No, it had not, s/he imagined, at his or her desk, no doubt it had not. But s/he could not remember,

now that it was over, there was a gap, there was a place without words, without images. There was the airport and no one to meet the plane, there was the shuttle bus to the city and no one there at the terminal, there was the solitary look down from above and there was the crowd far below and no one recognizable among the many people and then there was a gap, another gap, and they were in the street, and there was only the sky, ripped like a piece of paper, crumpled underfoot.

Other words, other images.

"It is all your fault. If you had wanted me to act in a certain way, you should have given me rules."

"I wanted love to be free."

"I wanted to get rid of you, once and for all. But then I discovered afterwards that I loved you more than ever."

S/he looked down at the concrete, where the sky was, in a new place.

III

At this particular point in the story s/he became the opposite of what s/he had been, such was the force of the event. In terms of visual perception nothing changed, as far as s/he could see. The rain was still the rain, a desk remained a desk, the office was the office. Other people did what other people had always done and not done at the office.

Only s/he had fallen into an impossible situation, that was all. The curious thing, however, was that no one at the office noticed. In their eyes s/he continued to do what s/he had always done at the office. S/he came in in the morning, s/he left at the end of the day, s/he did whatever s/he was given to do in between. S/he had always drawn a clear line between the private and the public. S/he was not about to cross the line.

What was peculiar was that life went on as if nothing had happened, when what one expected was actually the opposite of what happened, and what happened exactly what was not supposed to happen. But at the office no one noticed what had happened, or if anyone noticed anything out of the ordinary no one spoke of it, and that was the way it ought to be, s/he thought, since nothing could and should happen at the office, absolutely nothing.

IV

"They're asking me to break my principles," s/he announced, one day after work. "Then perhaps you should think of breaking them," replied the other, the other other, always ready to accommodate, always willing to go along.

S/he, however, refused to break his/her principles, whatever they were, and decided that under the circumstances it would be preferable, given what was happening, to change positions, at least temporarily, and so s/he took a job in another company, a higher position, it turned out, in accordance with the best rules of career management, and on an even higher floor, and with more window space, from which anyone could make out, far, far below, the geometry of the blackening streets, not to mention the distant blue hills of another state.

S/he knew at least what s/he was not going to do, now. S/he was not going to walk out of the office as the image of success, dressed in something like the best clothes that money can buy, and walk into the slums, even if the slums were only a step around the corner, there where the adult book shop visible from on high announced not only a change in what it meant to be an adult but a change in the function of the book itself, when s/he turned that corner s/he would be clad in the most ordinary of styles. That is the way a person walks the streets today, where the extraordinary has become the ordinary, the ordinary the extraordinary. Thus s/he would not see the man in the extraordinary clothes, if indeed it was a man, all s/he would see would be the pistol, attached to a hand, the black hole coming closer with every step each took toward the other. In the rain that in no way resembled prison bars or harp strings at the moment s/he would look into the barrel of the narrowing light and know that everything s/he was about to experience would have to be imagined.

Cuts

I

This is how they stole the funeral: they told stories. They were funny stories. They had to be. Everyone knew they had to be funny stories because everyone laughed even before they were told. A word or two and the room was full of laughter. They laughed and they laughed, the aunts and the uncles, the nieces and nephews, their husbands and wives, their children, cousins and the children of cousins. They laughed until they cried and then they cried until they laughed again. But first the video. It's all on video. So there they were, in the small space, the living room, in front of the blank of the screen. The first scene is a shock. I'm warning you. And there he was, in his box, the old man, the father, the brother, the uncle, the cousin, once and twice removed, he would not fit into the box, push as they pushed he would not go in. You'll see that it all works out in the end. Don't worry. And sure enough, at that moment, the body went in and the lid went over. Cut to the motorcade. Cut to the village. Cut to the speeches. What language can that be? Will you translate? You're good at languages. It must be French. It is not French. It is some horrible Colonial patois. It is their language. You can't blame them for that. Cut to the military salute: twenty-four black men, twenty-four guns. Cut to the dignitaries in their flowing robes, their caftans and their sandals. Look at the young men sitting in the rows behind them, the boys behind the young men. Ask yourself: Where are the women? Where are the girls? In the last rows. See? They are there.

II

Outside there was snow, outside there was silence. Everyone inside remarked how incredible the silence outside was. Or was it the snow they remarked because of the silence, rather than the silence on account of the snow, the silence which no sooner remarked no longer existed? How appropriate that the body would not go into the box. How like him to resist right up to the end. And that goatee. How like Colonel Sanders. He's lost weight. How enormous he looks. It is not easy to bury your father, your brother, your uncle, or your cousin, even once or twice removed. There was the snow, there was the silence. There were the stories. People were crying over the salmon, over the stories, the silence. Only the eyes of the orphans were dry.

III

It is all on video. Can I have a copy? There are no copies. Can you make us one? I can make each of you your own personal copy. Outside there was snow, outside there was silence. Inside the stories. The body would not go into the stories. Laughter, laughter. More and more laughter. Silence. We are such things as dreams are made on – not to be said. Not to be read. Put it away, the text, the chosen text. Cut to the stories, mouths moving, without words.

The Speech

Y must make a speech. Why Y? Why a speech? Because that's how it is, that's how it's done. But to whom must Y speak, and where, and in what language, and about what, that Y does not know. A speech must be made, somewhere, to someone, in some language, about something, and by Y, that much is clear, at least to Y, if Y is to make a speech, and not only to Y, for Y is not the only speaker in this world, of course, and were Y the only speaker in this world there would be no point in speaking, there would be no speech, and Y must make a speech, Y must say something. What Y must say is not yet known, at least not to Y, to whom the subject has not yet been given, and to whom even the language remains unknown. Thus how Y can say something is itself a mystery, at least to Y, who is not responsible for this state of affairs and who no doubt can only discover what he has to say in saying it, if not once he has said it, and thus, strictly speaking, no longer has it to say. And yet it is precisely the absence of what Y must say that most torments Y, it is this presence he cannot understand. No doubt this is part of the exercise, and a necessary part, if exercise it is, and not a test, for Y is after all applying for a vacancy. Y must therefore present himself, and not only Y, but all the people involved, as capable of filling this particular vacancy. Thus the words, thus the subject, thus the audience, even the language must remain unknown to Y, and not only to Y. No doubt some people would protest such a situation at once, if not in the name of human rights then in the principle of uncertainty itself, for not to know is itself a humiliation. But no doubt such a humiliation, if humiliation it is, is part of the test, if not the test itself, for anyone willing to accept humiliation cannot on principle object to humiliation, one's own or another's, and thus the not knowing, terrible as it may be, is itself the point, if point there is, and has to be endured, even without language, and whatever language it is or is not to be, as the test, the proof of which is its own taking, and thus this, too, must be considered part of the speech.

Breakthrough

U pushed open the door to the other room. The door was a door without a handle, in fact, there was nothing for the hands, it was a wonder anyone could find the way out, or in, so cunningly had the architect made the doors that were it not for the slight line nothing would have been visible, only the wall, and it was only by pushing against the wall that you discovered that this solid white world was not so solid after all. But instead of finding the other room for the night, as he had imagined, U found himself in a large open space crowded with people staring at him. After all, he was the person who had broken through the wall, that must be how they saw him now, and, unaccustomed to being stared at, U turned back to what for him was still a door, but the door had already closed, he had not even managed to get his briefcase into the new space. U pushed back against the white surface, only nothing happened, there was no door now, apparently, only the wall, at least from this side, not even the line or outline was visible. This new architecture is even more cunning than one thinks, U thought, pushing harder and even more in vain against the wall. There really was no going back, that was clear now, there was no going forward, either, so great was the crowd. Inside what U had taken at first glance to be a large open space turned out to be a small but elaborate theatre. People began to applaud as he tried to separate himself from the wall or the door or whatever it was he was leaving behind him. But the other room, he cried out, only in a whisper, and then, letting go, turned round and took his place among the others.

One of the Many

I hurried up the central street, in search of something for the holidays, but as he hurried up the street other people streamed toward him, as if in flight, and as I looked at and into the faces and in particular the eyes he, too, turned away, fleeing, and, one of the many, if only now by having turned his back, looked into the distance, or what was left of it, from which he had come, for the distance was exactly what was disappearing, and as I looked into what remained in front of him more and more people appeared, streaming toward him, with the same face, the same eyes, only now, one of the crowd as he was, I knew there was no turning back.

Mobile

They are in the streets, in trams and buses, wherever you turn, there they are, the voices, not meant for you. And what in the world is to be heard in all this wording? On the sidewalk, I am on the sidewalk. On the way to work, I am on my way to work. After work, I am on my way home. Singular confessions, more wanton wooings, most pitiful proposals. It is a crazy age, you tell yourself, if you say anything, everyone talking at once, everyone on the move, everyone in advance of themselves, and what is lost in all this language sharing is the silence, or what you took for the silence, a vision of your own, you say, the voice of vision, only to yourself, and then you see the truly lunatic, the local mad man with his booming sounds, his Biblical reminders and reproaches, his scraps of poetry so richly worn, gesticulating like a mad Shakespearian king as he steps forward toward you with the question: "How are you?" And before you can answer – for after a hard day's work you hardly know how or who you are – he adds, prophetically, and not without delight, if laughter can be read still as delight: "Just try and stay that way!"

All's Well

H is everything that a man should want, except rich: she is kind, she is generous, she is intelligent, she is beautiful, and she loves B and only B. But wealthy as he is B does not want to marry someone poor. When the authorities tell B nevertheless that he must marry H, for she has done the authorities a good turn, B realizes that he has no choice, the authorities being what they are, but decides not to consummate the marriage; and thus no sooner does he satisfy the authorities than he sends the woman now his wife to his mother, a widow and in need of company, he tells himself, and sets out to seek his fulfillment in war. Before he leaves her H extracts a promise that should he ever give her the family ring – something he has sworn not to do – and make her pregnant – something under the circumstances that can not even be imagined – he will return. B has made the promise in the full confidence that it will never be kept and departs for the wars, where, killing many human beings, he is recognized as a hero and admired by all who admire and recognize as heroic such behavior in a man. Informed of his actions, H announces her desire to make a pilgrimage to a sacred place, only to show up at the battlefront, in disguise, where she discovers that her hero husband is now heroically wooing D, another kind, generous, intelligent, and beautiful woman, who, like H once, is without financial means of her own but who, unlike H, does not love B. The now rich H works out a deal with D that will help D to overcome her one clear shortcoming: D agrees to accept B's advances, though only on a verbal level, and at the appointed time to let H take her place. After the consummation of her marriage, H has her death announced so that her husband in an illusion of perfect safety will come home. Only H has arranged to have the now rich D tell the authorities the truth and, pregnant and in possession of the family ring, which B had ceded as a pledge in the blindness of his passion, is herself produced as proof.

Poor B has no choice now but to admit the sins of his youth and, in front of everyone, to beg for forgiveness. This is not as you like it, there is too much plotting for a comedy of errors, and in our company, we have recently begun to offer alternative performances in which H and D change roles; this has proven so popular that we have begun to rotate the parts of B, H and D as well. It is clear what development this logic must lead to, and it is only a matter of time until all our roles become interchangeable, rich and poor, male and female alike.

Empire of Flies

The flies are on the glass, and, from where you are, you can not tell if they are on the outside, trying to get in, or on the inside, trying to get out, for they are simply there, like letters, letters in a liberation of language, letters which if legible at all can be read only because of what they do not represent, everything but themselves. Approach and they fly away, withdraw and they regroup their blacknesses, winged as they are, as if their possible significations, their origins, their etymologies themselves, were on the move, momentous darkenings, illuminated next-to-nothings, alight with their own obscurities, and calling attention, in their own particular way, to the translucent pane.

Immigrant Song

The bus doors open like the folds of an accordion and the people come out like notes. It is a clear autumn song of a day, light and shadow are equally mixed under the trees, and the leaves are falling like the notes themselves. This generation of the leaves is itself well-known, like the contrast of light and shadow, but no less real for being repeated. On a clear day the doors open and close like the folds of an accordion, and the immigrant song goes on, in the people, the leaves, the light, and the shadow, as far as the eyes, even closed, can see.

An Ordinary Life

1

"Finally," says the father.

"How was the film?" asks the mother.

"Ridiculous," says the daughter.

"You cried all the way through," says the young man at her side.

"That's what I mean by ridiculous."

"Was it a love story?" asks the mother.

"If you call that love."

"I wouldn't call that love."

"What would you call love?"

"I don't know what I would call love. But certainly not that!"

2

"What about dinner?"

"What dinner?"

"Your dinner?"

"We already ate dinner."

"Then why did you come here?"

"To sleep."

Father and mother look at each other.

"You came here to sleep?"

"We can talk if you'd like."

"About what?"

"The film," the daughter says, looking at her parents. "The love story."

3

"You can't sleep here."
"Why not?"
"Because there's only one bed."
"We only need one bed."
"But you aren't married."
"Neither are you."
"That's different. We were once."

4

The father clears his throat.
"I have something to say," he says.
"Then say it, simply."
"There is nothing to say," says the mother. "Under the circumstances, there is nothing to say."
"There is."
"There is not."
"Life is a journey on a darkening sea whose depths escape us just as surely as the spume evaporates into the air."
"And what is that supposed to mean?"
"It means," says the mother, "that a gentleman dissolves into his environment like sugar in hot water."
"Then someone else must do the stirring."
"Do not contradict your mother."
"And spume doesn't evaporate into the air," the daughter says. "It falls back into the sea. It falls back into the sea and disappears."

5

"What does he do?" the mother whispers, pulling her daughter aside.

"He's a painter," the daughter replies.

"A painter?" the mother cries out, shocked.

"A painter and a composer!"

"A composer?"

"And a magician, too!"

"What she's trying to say," says her father, "is that he hasn't got a job."

"What she's trying to say," his daughter replies, "is that he's a very talented person."

"Of course he is," her mother answers. "Otherwise she wouldn't have invited him home to meet us."

"I didn't invite him home to meet you. We went to the movies and afterwards we came here to sleep, because it is late and sleep is a biological imperative."

"Don't talk biology to me!" the mother says.

6

"He's gone!"

"Who's gone?"

"Your partner for the night."

"The love of my life!"

"How do you know?"

"Know what?"

"That he's gone."

"You chased him away."

"He may only be out for a walk."

"Not him. If there's one thing I know about him, it's that he's not the walking type."

"Maybe he's hiding somewhere."

"I don't go out with men who hide!"

"He's simply left you," says the father.

"Then it's not me he's left, it's you," says the daughter. "It's this whole horrible family."

"That's what men do," says the mother, looking at the one man left in the room. "They come and they go. They do what they want with us and then they leave us with the mess they have made."

"He hasn't made a mess. He hasn't done anything at all!"

"Typical artist!"

"He's not an artist," the young woman cries out. "He's just a person who wants people to think he has talent precisely because he has none. He's an ordinary person, in other words, and that's what makes him special, at least for me, and that's what you've taken away from me, the most beautiful thing in the world, an ordinary life, with an ordinary person!"

Without Title

1

"Why aren't you at your mother's side?"

"She asked me to leave," the young man replied, "so she could sleep."

"She's not asleep."

"She was when I left."

"If you look again," his uncle said, a look of triumph in his eyes, "you'll see that she's not."

The young man turned away to the window of the waiting room, and saw on the other side of the glass the other side of the hospital corridor.

2

Through the glass she could be seen, from waist to head, half a human being, moving back and forth in the corridor on the other side of the transparent waiting room wall, her cheeks rouged, her eyelids green and blue, the eye-brows black, but the line blurred, the lips scarlet, wet and scarlet, and heard, too, though the source of the sounds was not visible, the high heels marking time, unevenly, as she prepared to turn, his sister, a sudden staccato flurry in the eerie hospital silence, worried, serious, slowing down, reversing direction, acquiring speed to reach the other end of the corridor, now out of sight, and then to begin again, her face in a frown, solemn, fixed, as she moved in and out of sight like a target in an amusement park.

Then a doctor appeared, and she broke into smiles.

3

"This is a real chance for her," said Polly. "Don't you think so?"

"What sort of chance do you mean?"

"The only chance! For a woman – to get a husband! Here, at the hospital!"

"It's too late," said Wynn. "It's too late for that."

"What do you mean, *too* late? It's never too late, unless you think it is."

"Look at her make-up. She's hiding her age."

"What else has she got to hide? And if it works?"

"It never works!"

"A doctor – wouldn't that make your mother happy!"

"She's already happy," his uncle said. "Dying cheers her up."

Through the glass window the smile passed to the doctor's face. The young woman began to move her lips, quickly. Slowly, the doctor's smile turned to a frown, his lips moved, the frown was passed back to the young woman's face, distorted, immediately, into a smile, and then once again she was alone.

4

The older man announced:

"I'm going to tell him."

"Don't tell him!"

"I will!"

"You said you wouldn't!"

"I changed my mind!"

"You promised!"

"I'm free to change my mind!"

"Then go ahead!"

"Perhaps I shouldn't...."

"You said you would...."

"Alright, then I will!"

He turned and announced:

"If you need any money, don't turn to us!"

"What ever made you think I'd turn to you?"

"What?" his uncle said, shocked. "Who else can you turn to? Don't you know how much medical care costs in this country? After all, someone has to get rich. And don't expect anything from your father. He's been crying poorhouse ever since his mother died. How much do you think she left him? And all wasted! Money! Makes a man lazy! Ruins his character! Look at your father. Quit his job, left your mother, and now she can't even pay the insurance – and he's crying poorhouse!"

"He's got a new job," the older woman interrupted.

"Have you?" her husband exclaimed. "How much do you make?"

His nephew told him.

"I'm impressed!" he said, and lowered his voice.

In the silence, nothing could be heard but the clicking of heels in the corridor, alternate and uneven, and the rustling of paper in the waiting room, a topical magazine, already out of date.

5

The small room was crowded with people he did not know. All he could see of his mother was a mound under a white sheet. He approached the bedside and took her hand. "This is my son!" she cried out, but in a small voice. They looked into each other's eyes. "And this man," she said, smiling, and taking the hand of a person the son had never before seen, "would make an excellent husband for my daughter!" The stranger smiled back. "Forgive me," the mother whispered, pulling the son's ear to her mouth. "There's so little time, and I must take care of business first." "You were forgiven before I was born," the son said. "And your uncle? You must forgive him, too. He thinks he's a dog, you know. You should feel sorry for him." "A dog?" "He stood outside my bedroom door when he came to visit me and barked all night." "He came to visit you and barked all night?" "Yes. He asked if he could visit me and I didn't know that he thought he was a dog and so I said he could. What else could I say? I didn't know that he would bark all night outside my door." "What did he want?" "He wanted me to know how lucky I am to have a house of my own. You don't understand. You think he's rich and can't envy me anything. But he's lost his job, that's what we all think, all this talk of money is a fiction to hide the truth, he worked too much, that's all, he wore himself out and they let him go, and you know how they've always lived, beyond their means, so it's worse than being out in the street, at least that's rent-free, but they're going into debt, for nothing, they won't even be able to pay the psychiatrist, and when he called how could I refuse him, I sensed that something was wrong, something broken, I –

"My great stone belly!" she cried out, and clasped her hands over her large belly, as if she were pregnant with her last child.

"Time!" said the nurse.

6

The son bent over the fountain as the water rose like a flame.

"Money! What's wrong with money?" his uncle cried out, then fell to his knees, as if he were going to pray, and instead began to bark like a dog. "You mustn't think badly of him," his aunt said. "He has no job and I have cancer and there is no hope." "Dogs! Dogs!" his uncle cried out to the wall. "Listen," his mother's sister said, giving him the arm he should have taken himself and with her other hand pointing out the stranger in the leather motorcycle jacket he had seen at his mother's bedside. "Don't let your sister be seen like this. They just met today, by mistake, in the wrong room. And this is perhaps her last chance to get married."

The Lears

Nice people, the Lears, we said. From the old country. Bringing the benefits of the old ways to our new world. What we need here, the old values, the old traditions. And so we welcomed them with open hands. And the property those people could accumulate! The woods, the swimming pool, the helicopter pad, the English garden with its cottage and the heath! Look what the gardener is doing to the heath, we said. How natural the walk-ways have become. And what a view you get of the sea now from those beetle-browed cliffs, we added, before those paths were closed to us. And the father, we said. Now there is a father! Someone to respect. A single parent who can do it all. Strict, we had to admit. Strict, we said. Strict but generous. Look how the girls adore him. So we sent our girls out to play with his. That was a mistake, of course, as we saw later, much too late.

Then came the relatives. The Macbeths, Coriolanus and his mother, Gertrude and Claudius. Ambitious people. Great party-givers. And the talk! You couldn't sleep at night, it was so rhythmical. What syntax! What evasions! What shifts of meaning! Of course, it wasn't long before they all went into politics.

Character

"Work builds character," Work said, and everyone rose to applaud, even his wife on her frail legs.

"That is what my father said, and his father before him, and his father before that, and character – "

The old man began to choke and cough.

The banquet had clearly been too much for Work, the honors sat heavily upon his bony frame, even his dazzling white hair seemed about to fly off in all directions in the chaotic wind.

"Character, my dear friends, is what we want at work!"

Work sat down to even more applause, drank whatever was in his glass, recalled the body of his most recent mistress, thought of his father's heart attack on the 5:05 to Greenwich, and wiped his lips. His wife, who liked to boast that she had never changed a lightbulb in her life, let alone had to work, broke into tears. Work took the napkin from his lips, passed it to her, drew deeply on his cigarette, producing a round fiery glow, and stared stonily at the ash-white sky beyond the garden.

"I have been a bad father and a worse husband," Work admitted, only in a whisper, so that even his daughter at his side was not sure that she had heard the old man mumbling rather than imagined the words. "For once we agree," she replied, not knowing if indeed he could hear her above the shouts and silences. The old man wrinkled his nose, as if in the presence of something unsavory. "You have to respect your father. After all, he's a wonderful man," said Mrs. Work, afraid that something like a scene was about to develop. She wiped away the ashes on her husband's lapel and nudged her daughter pointedly in the ribs. "Ask him about work. That's what he likes to talk about. That's what all men like him like to talk about."

"And what about you?" said a bald-headed man with a snake-like imprint on his pate, bending over the young woman and following down with his eyes the line between her breasts.

"What do you do?"

"She's only beginning to work," her father announced, with a full voice now, and no trace of a cough. "So don't ask what she does, ask what she will do. For whatever she does today, tomorrow she will do something more. Whatever she does tomorrow, the next day she will do something else. Thus the present disowns the past for the future, which does not exist, and becomes the past, which is of no use."

Work took back the napkin from his wife to dry his forehead, looked at the stony sky for longer than he realized, and saw that the snake-marked man and his daughter had withdrawn together into the shadows of the fruit trees.

"I shall disinherit her at once," Work whispered, waking his wife, and, closing his eyes so as to see nothing unsuitable, continued to think about work.

The Day of Forgiveness

It is the day of forgiveness. The people line up in the little square in spite of the rain and forgive each other. Lovers forgive each other, whole families come together and forgive each other, the representatives of governments local and national forgive each other, the leaders of foreign countries send their emissaries, even the heads of religions forgive each other and themselves for what their religions have done and not done to the others. "I did not know," says one. "I knew and did nothing," says another. "What I did I should not have done." "What I should have done I did not do." "Try to forget," says one. "Forgive and forget," says another. "I will forgive but I will never forget," says another. "I may forget, from time to time, I may need to forget," says still another, "but I will never forgive." There is a space, too, in which no one speaks, a space apparently to be avoided, a dirt space apart from the speeches in which no one is to stand, a place, it is said, for those who have no voice, and whose silence alone can be heard only in the void and only without voice, a silence which, if heard, others say, is neither void nor voice, but something beyond words. There are lawyers, too, in the crowd, listening, speaking of compensation for what others say is and should be forever beyond compensation. The lawyers, of course, have to be forgiven, too, according to the logic of the day, and by the same logic so have those who insist that there is and can be no compensation, as well as those who always refuse to take part at all in such ceremonies, who shut their doors on the public display of grief and guilt, who say with or without voice there is nothing to be said, nothing to be done, that we must bear alone our differences in silence till we die.

A Wild and Wonderful World

The shadows fall like pieces of metal. They cut if you are not careful. They cut even if you are. But if you wait too long the whole city goes under. Already the flood is beginning, darkening everything. One foot, then, in front of the other, then the other, always the other, the other other, back now drawn forward, one step at a time. There is nothing to this. That is the strange thing. The lines of the street narrow to nothing, the architecture vanishes, and then it is night. One step and then the other. Always the other. Now that the shadows were everywhere, there were no shadows. That was the strange thing. Wherever you put your foot, there was the concrete, there were the cracks in the concrete. Not to fall in. Not to be crushed. You have to be a colossus not to fall in, not to be crushed. Walk on your own feet, then, and tell yourself, whatever happens, it is going to be a wild and wonderful world.

Late at Night

The Summons

It is late at night, and only the lights of the station can be seen when you step from the train into the darkness. How will he recognize you in all this darkness, the coachman, among all these passengers, you ask yourself, emerging from the car only to see that there are no other passengers at the station. There is not even a station master. Is there a coachman, you wonder, looking first to the left, then to the right, and discovering the man directly in front of you. He bows, or seems to bow, an old man, though it is only his head that makes the effort, now, opening the door then before closing it once you have climbed the single, solitary step and taken your place inside. Then the darkness that had seemed so immovable begins to move: a tree, trees, the lake, a house, disappear, one by one; other trees appear, other houses, then a wall. The coach stops. The door opens. You step outside. Someone bows, you see only half a figure, someone else opens a door out of the dark into a surprise, a corridor of light. Someone else bows, someone in gold braid. You notice men in pointed helmets, sentinels, inside the corridor, the corridors, as far as you are made to walk, and then another door is opened by still another man in gold braid, and there, inside the room, inside the suite of rooms, your rooms, the servants wait; one lights the fire, the other out of nowhere sets the table: cold meats and *petits fours*. Then they withdraw. Alone at last, you do what you have always done when you are on your own: go to the window, draw the curtains, and look out. There is the simple truth in front of you: the long illuminated façade of the imperial palace, the guards patrolling in the darkness, rifles on their shoulders, and beyond the guards, somewhere inside the palace, somewhere inside one of the rectangles of light, if not already in darkness, waits the one and only human being, the empress herself, who has summoned you all this way to read.

Bridge of Bones

To enter the country you must cross a bridge of bones, and from whatever frontier you have chosen, ribs, feet, fingers, arms and legs, backbone and skull, dismembered and remembered into a series of commemorative, historical arches suspended above the waters raging all the way to the capital itself deep within the heart of the nation. The bones are those of enemies, internal and external, it is said, those defeated in battle to establish the nation in the first place, those defeated in battle in defense of the nation afterward, those enslaved to make the country what it is and those who revolted against such practices, outlaws and criminals, former friends and feckless foes, those who have found their final resting place under the motto emblazoned at the entrance and exit of each bridge: Don't tread on me, or I will tread on you. Thus the bridge of bones, thus the statement, clear and distinct, to all those who from outside the reverent borders even dream of crossing over into the territory, and thus the necessary and sufficient and long-acclaimed ritual in this country of bridges for all young people, male or female, as they cross over into adulthood: to walk half-way across the bridge, unaided and alone, without once looking down into the abyss below.

Guards and Prisoners

Our criminal justice system does not work. This is the opinion of experts on both sides of the political spectrum, though the solutions proposed to reform the system, coming as they do from both sides of the spectrum as well as from people who claim to represent the center, differ wildly, as is to be expected in a situation where extremes are inevitable. Recently, however, we who work within the system have made an important change in and indeed a significant contribution to the model of reform: we have begun to recruit our prison guards from within the prisoners themselves. This lowers resistence to internal surveillance, at least in theory, among the prisoners, increases the democratic character of our most important and defining institution, and significantly reduces costs. No wonder, then, that such a reform has been greeted with such wild acclaim, not only within the prison itself but outside our walls as well and even abroad. In fact, people have begun to apply for positions within the prison, so many that we now have a waiting list of potential residents. The implications of such a procedure have not been lost on the international community, for whom we have become a model, as well as on our local authorities: Control yourself, that is what we say, in public and in private, and discipline will take care of itself. Be your own guard, your own prisoner.

Memorial

"What you are looking at," said the guard, looking at the wooden barracks in their rows, beyond which could be seen, in reverse, the black and famous words, WORK MAKES YOU FREE, "is nothing other than a reconstruction of the camp, albeit as exact a one as could be made. The original was destroyed." "But why would you destroy the original?" I asked, refusing as he always did to read the guidebook in advance. "Because of the memories," the guard said. "Then why were they rebuilt?" "For the same reason," the guard replied.

Variations on a Theme

A boy whirled about in the parking lot of a shopping mall. Each time he completed his counter-clockwise circle he bowed to the blackness of the lot and snapped the fingers of his right hand, first to the left, in front of him, then to the right, before straightening his lithe little body and continuing his circular dance. "What are you doing?" asked an old man who had stopped to watch the boy. "What does it look like I'm doing?" the boy replied, impatiently. "I'm dancing to keep the country free of Indians." "But there are no Indians," the old man said, sadly, and smiled, or tried to smile. "You see," the boy said, proudly, as if he were an element in the local defense, and no small element at that.

Bellevue

Joan walks to the window and looks down on the city. "It could be as beautiful as a garden of flowers in France," she says, observing the pattern of the streets, "the walkways in the garden of geometry. No wonder that the place is called Bellevue. But now everything is burning," she adds. "Can you not see that everything is burning?" "I see nothing," says the page. "Why don't you keep a record and write down what you see?" "Nothing is ordinary," Joan replies, paying no attention to the page, and looking down at everything in smoke and flames. "But you must commit yourself," she goes on. "That is the secret. That is the way things work. That is the truth, the order of the day. They can not commit you. Not even your own family can commit you now. Can you not see the flames? Can you not see that everything is burning?" But the page makes no response. The page has gone blank. "The whole city is on fire. And more than the city. The age itself is burning. I am Joan of Arc, I must go out into the world. And when I do, they will catch me, eventually they will catch me and betray me and hand me over to the enemy, who will tie me to the stake, their whore and heretic. Already I can feel the fire flickering. I can see the ash, the arc, the trajectory I must become."

Black Knight

I must put on my armor, I can not put on my armor: thus the dilemma, right from the start. I who am to lead the army to recover the Holy Land can not even mount my own horse. How humiliating for a man of my stripe and stature to have to stand here, below the tree, dwarfed by a horse, waiting for others to hoist him into herodom. Greaves, breast-plate, helmet, shield emblazoned with stars – such are the appurtances of my life, my fate. Not to forget the plume, my feather, plucked from the egret's wing. Let it provide a signature, my signature, before I begin to write, in blood, the other story.

Without End

I

He lay in bed and thought about his work, the way the taxi moved
in straight lines, a left turn or a right, the destination annihilated the
moment it was reached, the end the beginning of something else,
another person, another possibility, connecting spots of time through
lines in space, and what you do and have to do at night, he told himself,
is find a rhythm of your own and ride it out.

II

"What happened?"
"A collision."
"Was it your fault?"
"Another car ran a red light."
"I'm not going to help you."
He turned from the woman to the wall.
"I don't want you to get the wrong idea of me."
"What is the wrong idea?"
"That I'm someone you can depend on."

III

"Of course, I'm grateful," she went on, after a pause, looking at the
slanted broken mirror that covered the hole in the floor through wh=ich
glowed the light from the illegal carpentry shop below.
"For what?"
"For everything. You gave me my personality."

"Don't be a fool," he replied. "Nobody gives anybody anything like that."

"Only gratitude does not engender love, it engenders hatred."

He closed his eyes and obliterated what remained of her. But even with his eyes closed he could see her moving past the toilet in the hall, walking down the steps in the darkness, pushing open one door and then the next, then looking at the body bags of garbage in the street. In another world there were elevators, going up and down. He could see the doors opening and closing, opening and closing. She raises her hand like a schoolgirl, a taxi screeches to a stop. She climbs into the back seat and gives the driver a destination, then sits back to wait for the office buildings to rise into view. The driver sets the meter like a clock, looks in the mirror overhead at the woman now in his care, notes where he has to go on the trip-tick provided for no other purpose, plots as required by the laws of the profession the shortest distance between two points, and then, slowly, inevitably, accelerates.

A Place of Your Own

The street was deserted when U approached the number he had been given by the real estate agent. Music was playing from somewhere inside the building. That is a bad sign, U thought, early in the morning as it is, although of course it is always possible that the listener and I can come to terms, even reasonable terms, regarding rights and disturbances, and at any rate U had to work throughout the day so music during office hours was not going to be a problem. The night, of course, was another story. After a hard day at work U for one needed sleep. But when U approached the door of what should have been the apartment building he saw that the number above his head on the pane of glass did not correspond to the number that he held in his hand. That is peculiar, U told himself, looking into the narrow interior corridor at the flaking paint, and then, stepping back into the street, he saw that the number he was seeking was actually to the left of the entrance of the apartment building, above a small and narrow door. The window next to it was absurdly large, at least in comparison to the size of the door, though what the window masked U could not tell, for a pink curtain had been drawn across it from inside. This must be the place I am looking for, U thought, dubious as it seemed. In front of him there was an old man rummaging through the transparent garbage bags. U side-stepped the person and looked for a buzzer, but there was no buzzer, so as if it were the most ordinary act in the world, as if U were a familiar guest or even already a resident of the building, he pushed open the door. There was no music now, he realized, as soon as he had stepped inside, as if his own appearance had put an end to whatever had been going on without him. In the interior darkness nothing was clear. Only once his eyes had grown accustomed to the lack of light did he discover that he was in a large empty room. There were tables scattered about, in no apparent order, but with the chairs all facing the same way. Without thinking of what he was doing he found himself looking in the one direction, as if he were one of the absent spectators himself, and saw that there was something like a stage backed by a hall of mirrors. At the table closest to the stage a woman sat dressed in what looked like nothing, drinking something out of a tall glass. To the far right, and almost lost in shadow, an old man stood behind the counter of a bar staring out into the distance as if there were something there to see. This is certainly not what you had in mind for a place of your own, U thought. Nevertheless you can not simply walk in and then walk out again without a word. You must say something. But as U stepped forward, not knowing to whom he should address whatever he was going to say, the music began to play, as if connected to the movement of his body; the woman at the table put down her drink, climbed on to the stage, with some difficulty, it seemed to the young man, and began to dance, shedding piece by piece what little clothing she was actually wearing. There must be some mistake, U cried out, if only to himself, and with these words, or something like them, turned his back on the older man and woman. At that moment the music stopped as abruptly as it had begun, though in the cessation of the singing the sound of his own voice continued to resound, at least in his own ears, as the silence fell on U like a rebuke.

Schoolmaster Massys

Schoolmaster Massys, that massive man, sits at his desk in the teachers' room, his mastiff at his feet, preparing the final exams. The teachers have been told by the director of the school that all the pupils are to pass the test, even little Colin, who, though not dumb, at least not in the eyes of Schoolmaster Massys, simply refuses to study and who in consequence has never passed a single examination. "It is not fair," she has told the teachers, "it is not fair if the boy fails again." "But it is not fair to the others," Massys replies, but only once he realizes that no one else in the room is going to speak up. "It is not fair to those who have done the work if those who have not are accorded the same results. If you take away the possibility of failure," he goes on, to the astonishment of everyone in the room, "not only success, but achievement, work itself, will lose its meaning, and thus our lives as teachers of the young." In the silence that accompanies these words Massys sees that with every word he is uttering he is binding himself down with countless invisible but nevertheless real threads and that, if anyone is to fail now, and in this place, it is bound to be himself.

The Most Beautiful Woman in the Room

1

"The point is to please," the mother said, adjusting the cross-like bow in her daughter's hair, and smiling, so that everyone in the room could see her unnaturally white teeth. Recorded music came from the further room. "That's the truth! The truth," she cried out, as if precisely because of its doubtfulness it was necessary for her to repeat the words. The girl began to cry. "Truth isn't pleasant," the father said, pointing a finger menacingly if not toward his daughter then toward his wife. "You'll wake the dead," he added. The mother let the bow go and not looking at her husband walked into the next room, where the corpse lay. At once everyone rose and followed her. Around the open coffin stood the mourners, talking. The corpse lay on its back, the fingers interlaced upon the breasts, red rouge on the taut cheeks. "The most beautiful woman in the room," Petrov said, himself an elderly gentleman, and a lifelong bachelor. "One of the traditions we've kept," the mother explained. "The open coffin. The old country." Petrov took the hand of the dead woman and kissed it. An elderly woman approached the father of the little girl. "Rolls Royce. You're with Rolls Royce, now, aren't you?" she asked. "You must be a happy man. A happy man!" Petrov, himself deeply moved, bowed deeply. "I'd pay you just to let me wash the floor of your car." "The most beautiful woman in the room," Petrov repeated. "My own mother," the younger woman muttered, turning to the wall. "My own mother – and I wouldn't even recognize her!"

2

The corpse was waiting for them at the church. The immediate family took their places in the first row of pews. The priest began to read.

He read in the language of the deceased, and as he read an elderly acolyte distributed candles from a cardboard box and then moved among the mourners lighting them. Occasionally the priest would pause, as if waiting for something from his audience, but no one knew what was expected, if anything was expected, unless it was Petrov, who, at the back of the church, could not be seen without everyone turning from the altar. Finally, in the increasingly long silences, the acolyte began to gesture with his hands for the mourners to kneel, or rise, the old palms pressing downwards or upwards against the air. Then somewhere out of sight a cantor began to sing. The acolyte, lifting the empty cardboard box, gestured with it toward the altar. But the mourners did not know what to do. Then the old acolyte raised a last unlit candle from the box and pointed to the candleholder. A child rose, other people followed, carrying their light forward. The child tried to fit the candle into the hole. But the candle would not fit. Her father tried to make the candle fit by forcing it, but all he produced was a series of wax shavings. Other people tried to fit their candles to the holes, but they, too, failed, the holes were too small. Soon the wax began to melt. It slipped down the candles onto people›s hands. The cantor stopped singing. «I can›t believe this,» the mother said. The girl laughed. The father slapped her face and then there was silence in the church. The cantor began another hymn. «I›ll teach you to behave,» the mother whispered, tightening the bow. «I›ll teach you to behave if I have to kill you.» The acolyte pointed the unlit candle beyond the altar toward a further candleholder. There the holes were of the necessary shape and size. Slowly, without candles, their flesh scarred, the mourners returned to their places. Then the priest began to read in English from the Bible. As he read, the acolyte moved quickly back and forth, more and more desperately, between the altar and the door, his palms beating upwards or downwards to lift or lower the people. «No sense of protocol,» said the daughter of the dead woman as she rose as commanded and approached her mother. Petrov was already at the coffin›s edge. He took the corpse›s hand in his and then kissed the lips one last time. «Disgusting,» said the daughter. «They should hand out programs. Why can›t they supply notes?»

3

Outside it was raining. By the time the mother and child had reached the street where the limousines were waiting everyone else was standing on the concrete under umbrellas. "What is everyone waiting for?" said the mother. "The dead," came the answer. "The dead go first. Now they are carrying the coffin out." "So that's how it's done," she whispered, in astonishment. There was the sound of a door closing. "How could I know?" The hearse began to move. Soon they were all moving, inside, away from the church and through the concrete of the city, past the new shopping center and into the suburbs to the cemetery. "Why is it called Mount Hope?" the girl with the bow asked as they entered the iron gates. "It has to have a name," the mother answered. "Why are you so curious?" Professionals with black umbrellas were waiting for them at the grave. Once they had gathered again more words occurred, then in the silence the dirt was thrown onto the coffin. It made a hollow sound. "Take a handful of earth," the mother said to the girl as they approached the hole and looked down at the coffin. Only then did she notice that the cross was not of the form she had ordered. "How terrible!" she cried out, only in a whisper, as she pulled the young girl back from the pit's edge. "Oh, well," she added. "Who'll know the difference?"

A Dog's Life

1

All the children in the family called him Kent, though Kent was not his real name, and what impressed us children most about the man was the fact that he had once written Superman comics. My parents thought this was an unworthy occupation for an adult, a ridiculous way for a man to make a living. But Uncle Kent had not needed to earn a living, at least not before he married my mother's sister. He had inherited a substantial sum of money on the death of a man he had not known but who, he had come to think, must have been his father. Uncle Kent had grown up in England, in a castle not far from Kent, we were told, at the edge of a forest, and the man who had left him the money had lived in another castle on the other side of the forest, and for a while, as a child, I would make up stories about castle life at night when I could not sleep because of the shadows of the tree outside my window scrawled on the wall above my bed by the lights of quickly passing cars. What happened to the money I never learned: a house on a California beach, another in Florida, a penthouse apartment in New York, something in the Hamptons – this was how my mother saw things, or, rather, the gradual disappearance of things.

2

When I was old enough to visit my aunt and uncle alone in the City my uncle had lost all his money – "lost" was my mother's word – and was living in a small cluttered one-bedroom apartment on the East Side of Manhattan with his wife, my mother's youngest sister, and their dog, a white Pomeranian. He now had a job, something which my mother called an improvement, at least for my aunt: he worked for the telephone company in their public relations department. I remember a poster in the kitchen showing row after row of telephones arranged one to a square like the letters in an old-fashioned print box: these were the chronological advances that had been made year after year in the progressive improvement of telephone models, and this apparently was the fruit of my uncle's labors. When I asked my aunt where the Superman comics were, she gave me an alarmed look – even as a child I knew it was an alarmed look – told me they were in the closet, and then warned me never again to bring up the subject.

3

The last time my uncle visited us in the country he had become a dog. "He has lost his job," my mother whispered to us in her bedroom. "You should feel sorry for him." We did feel sorry for him, each in our own way, but at the same time we all were frightened, for we had never seen our mother hide herself in her bedroom with her children behind a bolted door, nor had we ever heard a human being bark like a dog, uncle or no uncle. "I am a dog," Uncle Kent cried out, in between the barks. "You are not a dog," my mother replied, doing what she could to maintain the semblance of human conversation. "You are a man who has lost his job." "I am a dog that has lost his master," my uncle barked back. "And I will stay here and bark all night long until you give me a place to stay." "You refused to help us when I was in hospital," my mother cried back. "So why should I help you now that you are not yourself?" "Because I was not myself then," my uncle cried. "But I am now."

The Mans

Mrs. Man took the scissors that she kept in the drawer under the telephone and cut the image out that she wanted to save from the magazine she had just thrown away. The image was an advertisement for a product and the product was the magazine she had just read showing on its cover the interior of a kitchen much like her own where a telephone had been screwed into a wall below a bulletin board hanging from a nail. Mrs. Man was good at cutting out things. She took the cut-out she had made without once lifting the scissors from the page and tacked it to the bulletin board above the telephone using the thumbtacks that she kept in the drawer below the telephone for no other purpose. "A wife should care about her husband's work," that was what Mrs. Man had told her daughters, from their infancy, preparing the girls for the real world. The girls, no longer girls but women now, continued to show no interest whatsoever in what their mother called the real world. "A wife should care about her husband's work," Mrs. Man repeated to herself, alone in the kitchen. Mrs. Man's father-in-law, Mr. Man's father, Mr. Man Sr., like his son, Mr. Man Jr., had been an advertising man, but his wife, Mrs. Man Sr., had not cut out her husband's work and tacked it to the bulletin board, not even in the early days of their marriage, when life was full of promise, and the marriage had ended in disaster. Mrs. Man Jr. had always said that she cared about her husband's work, unlike her mother-in-law, Mrs. Man Sr., for whom she did not care at all. She had tacked everything that her husband had written to the bulletin board above the telephone from the first days of their marriage, when love was full of promise, and she had gone on tacking the work to the board even after the marriage had ended in disaster. Was it not love but perhaps revenge, her daughters would ask, years later, too late, much too late, the former Miss Man and the current Ms., when the magazine had ceased to exist, the bulletin board had vanished, and even the walls of the house had disappeared.

Split-Level Development

One day the Colonel (who was not a colonel) barricaded himself behind the door of the master bedroom of his house, sat down alone on the double bed, drew across his lap a double-barreled shotgun none of us knew he had, and waited for the army to arrive. I don't know why my uncle expected the army to arrive; I don't know why he had a gun – we all lived in a split-level development, far from the woods and the migrating birds; and there was not a single hunter in the family. I only remember being told as a child that the Colonel and the government did not see eye to eye concerning the Panama Canal, and that my uncle, the husband of my father's sister, had decided that the time had come to take a stand on principle, no matter the personal cost. I had been brought up to admire a stand on principle, and so I found myself not without a certain if confused respect for my uncle's behavior, even if it was to cost him both his gun and his wife. The Colonel had been an inventor before becoming a bedroom defender of principle. He came from what my father condescendingly called "an old family", as if there were nothing quite so bad in this new age as coming from old stock, and there was my uncle, as proof, barricaded behind the bedroom door, of what could happen to a man who rested on his family laurels until they dried and cracked, refusing to go out, day after day after day, as my father did, to make his living at the office.

For the Sake of a Song

When Telemachus grew old enough to have some understanding of what had happened to take his father away from the family and leave him alone with his mother in the large and deserted house, he booked a passage on a boat and sailed to the island where, so he had been told, the friend of the father he had lost was now to be found. To the surprise of the young man, he found the old man exactly where he was said to be, and, equally surprising, in the arms of a young woman, hardly older than Telemachus himself. Perplexed by the sight of such an old man and such a young woman together, and not knowing how in the presence of the young woman to address the old man, who had drawn the bedsheet up to his nose as if to signal his withdrawal from the scene as well as his reluctance to speak of anything under the circumstances, at least with someone so familiar, and who was otherwise acting as if nothing out of the ordinary were happening and certainly nothing worth talking about with another human being, familiar or not, the young man turned to the woman and in his perplexity found himself asking her why everything that had happened had had to happen. She said it was all for the sake of a song.

On the Other Side

You can not see her, on the other side, when you enter her space, so she can not tell you not to enter her space, or to enter, as the case may be, for her back is to you, not her face, her back it is that faces everyone here at the office. Of course, the view is fantastic, face or no face. On this there can be no doubt. No wonder that she wants to enjoy the view here at the office. No wonder that she sits where she does, on the wrong side of the desk, at least according to the rules, with her back to us, so that she can look out, not at the world of the office but at the world outside the office. And she is an attractive woman, even from the back, that is the consensus of the men at the office, we do not hold back on our judgment here, she is attractive, no doubt about it. So why doesn't she want to face the world, our world, the world of the office, that is what we people ask, behind her back, that is what we want to know. It is a mistake, of course, but as a new employee she can not know, uninformed as she is, that not only the purchase but also the placement of all office furnishings is controlled by the Production Manager, and that in his eyes, and not only his eyes, the chair is on the wrong side, and not only the chair, the drawers are now on the wrong side, too, and drawers should not be on the wrong side of any human being. At least so she is informed by the Director, even if there is nothing in the drawers that she actually needs for her work, at least not at the moment; and if the need were to arise, so she says, all that she has to do is to walk to the other side. This, too, is a mistake, of course, a distinction of an individual need or nature not to be tolerated in our company, so says the Director, in her office, a corner office, the largest office in the company. It has two walls of windows, not one, and the Director's desk has been placed at a slant, with the Director between the windows and the desk, on the right side, in other words, and the surprising thing, and this is what the visitor sees as soon as she takes her place opposite the

Director in the visitor's chair, the surprising thing is that in such a position it is the visitor who can best enjoy the view. And the view is fantastic, even more fantastic, she has to admit, in the Director's office. "You
are on the wrong side," the Director says, as soon as the young woman
has sat down. "It's the right side for me," the young woman answers.
"But not," says the other woman, "for us."

The Line

The line had been drawn, unknown to myself, in the middle of the corridor and it was our task, each day, on entering the office, to walk the line to our respective offices. There were cameras mounted on the walls, of these I was aware, and above the doors, too, as well as in each individual office, which, among other things, recorded our linear progressions and deviations. As a new employee I could make no sense of any of these details, nor could I be expected to understand whatever purpose or plan such an arrangement might serve. The individual offices at our company open to the left and to the right alike, a simple system of symmetry is followed throughout the building, independent of personal preference. As a new employee I had been assigned a space in the interior. One day, toward noon, the telephone rang. It was my Supervisor. I was to come to his office at once. "This will never do," he said, rising, before I could even enter the office, and, taking a pointer like a schoolmaster at a blackboard, began to draw an imaginary line over the far wall. At almost the same time a film began to run. All the doors to the offices at our company must be kept open, this is an unwritten law, known to all, regardless of position, if voiced by none, and as I watched myself walking in an apparently haphazard fashion, no doubt exaggerated by the camera angles, swaying from left to right and from right to left, as if drunk, I could also see other members of our staff sitting at their desks. "You are going to tell me that they are augmenting the meager salary we pay them by doing outside work on company time. That may or may not be true," he added, before I could say a word. "But let me remind you that, whatever we do here," and here he looked gravely at me, but not without the trace of a smile, as if what he was about to say was for my own good and in fact the secret of success.

"Whatever we do, we walk the line."

Walls

A graffiti contest must be held in our city, the art dealers insist upon nothing less, pointing out that graffiti has become an international style, appropriate to our age, and as such commercially viable, for it is a style which anyone can learn, hence exclusive to no one, and yet this very style, appropriate as it is, at least in theory, and indeed the hallmark of our freedom, it is argued, at least abroad, is exactly the style which within and indeed upon the walls of our city the city authorities have forbidden and in fact outlawed. Walls should be blank, it is said, blanks pierced only by store windows, and if decorated then by the owners themselves and if not by the owners then for the owners, and for this work professionals exist, the graduates of our schools, people who respect commerce. Otherwise, why would they have paid to go to our schools in the first place? Graffiti is the signature of subversion, it is argued, at least by the authorities, and subversion is exactly what the authorities cannot tolerate if they wish to remain in authority. Such is the argument one hears today. Yet even those in authority feel the impulses of the age, for everyone knows that art is the sign of a civilized people, and we people will not be thought barbarians, at home or abroad. Thus walls have been created, walls in the open, walls where none are needed, walls which thus meet with the approval of the authorities in question, walls which can be removed to the galleries as soon as the work has been finished and the streets thus freed so that in our city nothing will have happened, nothing will have taken place.

Tablets

The old man raised the tablet and smashed it on the floor. No one seemed surprised by this action, no one seemed even to notice the act, the last he would perform in our spaces. And what did it matter, after all? We had our work. What he was destroying, we said, was not what had been written, for what we had to write on our tablets would be automatically deleted at the given time, but the possibility of writing itself. For such are the commands today. Another outraged office worker, we said to ourselves, if we said anything, turning back to our desks to do what we had to do, and refusing to see before us anything other than what we had always seen.

The Giraffe in Winter

The giraffe lifts his head above the trees. It is winter and this far north a giraffe has no choice but to live on air. We see him only in the daytime, his long neck poking through the tree-tops, taking in the light, the hairs on his outrageous head sprouting like twigs, his long legs hidden by the trunks of trees. He has escaped his predators, he has escaped the great savanna of his origins, the desert of his destiny, that unholy heat, and stands there in the Christmas cold looking at us as we sip our morning coffee as if we were the ones in need of consolation.

The Doomed and Damned

The messenger knows that he will be killed the moment he delivers the message. So why deliver it? Why be a messenger? Is the message so important? After all, everyone knows that the war has been lost, everyone knows that the empire is collapsing, and everyone knows that the barbarians for all their barbaric behavior are not altogether barbarians but people in their own right with a culture of their own. Why, then, deliver the message? Will not the truth arrive, all by itself, if it is the truth; and, if it is not, why mount the horse, if there is still a horse, why walk and crawl the long way home alone, why suffer the hunger and the hardship and the humiliation of such work, the doubts, the distances and darknesses, only to bring false comfort to the doomed and damned?

In the Natural Darkness

Everyone was working in the natural darkness, brightly and uniformly lit in accordance with the rules and regulations of the place.

"I'm looking for a job," I announced to the older man I took to be the one in charge.

"We're only looking for happy people," he replied, suspiciously, as if there were something wrong in the mere fact of wanting work.

Indeed, when I looked at the salespeople in the shop, I saw that everyone in the place was smiling fiercely.

"Do I look so unhappy?" I laughed, staring into the artificially lit darkness, but to no avail, for the man in charge had already turned his back and in the bright and windowless space was attending to the customers with a fierce smile of his own.

Museum Piece

You are in a new art museum. You have come here to look at the pictures, but as you approach the work you have chosen a man flies by on roller skates. Are you making this up, you ask yourself, for, after all, you have been working hard recently, too hard, you tell yourself, as usual, much, much too hard. But by the time these thoughts have formed the room is empty, as if absolutely nothing had happened. Then another figure on roller skates speeds by, if it is another figure and not the first again, in a recurrent dream, only a woman this time, you tell yourself, though by the time these thoughts occur the figure has already vanished without a trace. A love story? Why not? Who can tell? As you step toward the wall to view the painting that you want to see another skater races past, this time certainly a woman, to judge by the length of the hair, and followed by a man, if not the original, and in apparent pursuit of her. They must be good skaters to skate as they do. But will they not fall in this odd space? And what if they lose their footing and crash into a wall? Will not a work of art be damaged if not destroyed? Will not another human being, an innocent spectator, possibly, be hurt? But there is no one in the room, no one in the museum, it would seem, only yourself, alone, in a room of pictures, and the skaters as they skate past again and again. What speed, what balance, what supreme control, you tell yourself. There are four of them, you decide, two men and two women, if not two couples, engaged in some kind of competition, and in pursuit each of the other. Suddenly, one of the men stops at your feet, as if wanting a word, only to remove his jacket and hang it on the hand of the naked statue that in your distraction you have overlooked, a marble whiteness. Is this acceptable? Should a work of art be turned into a clothes rack? Is there no guard to prevent the desecration of what is after all public property? You are no caretaker, certainly, neither of the public nor of its property, but think of the precedent, for now that one skater has removed his jacket the others have followed suit. Is there no one to complain? No one to protest? No one to step forward to reclaim the silence and the sanctity of the place? By the time these thoughts have shaped themselves in your mind the roller skaters are roller-skating naked past the statue of the goddess clad in their clothes. I would like to point out something, you say, to the guard, somewhat shyly, not wanting to make a scene or a complaint or protest at all and not really knowing how to address the guard you have finally found, asleep at his or her post, and no doubt somewhat put off by the military-style uniform with its central row of brass buttons like a stutter of sunlight on dark water. But the guard seems not to understand what you are saying, or trying to say, at least the other gives the impression of not understanding, of not even listening, not even when you do what you can to translate the little that you have to say from one language into another, as if you might actually find a tongue where the other is at home, only to fail, once more, as if each word were, ultimately, the wrong word, as if the silence itself were out of order now.

The Blowing of the Horn

The angel put the trumpet to his lips and blew the horn. At the sound of the angelic call, and it was not a pleasant sound at all, but something harsh and altogether unmusical, every single individual within hearing distance, and it must have been a vast distance, indeed, to judge by the numbers, dropped whatever it was that they had been doing and assembled one by one at the feet of the angel, who, the better to be seen and heard, had climbed on to a pedestal in the shape of a broken column supporting nothing but the bluest of skies. "Why have we been called?" asked one of the many, and indeed the person closest to the angel, trying to maintain a distance from the others. "Because of the love you have betrayed," replied the angel from his pedestal, including the observer in the crowd. "But there is no one here who has not been called," said the observer. "That," said the angel, "is the punishment."

In the Clearing

They came out of the woods, screaming. It was happy screaming, from what I could tell. If anyone was to be unhappy, I thought, I was going to be that person. "There are no more men," said one, looking not so much at me as through me. "Of course, there are no more men," I replied. "Haven't you read the book? You are a tribe of Amazons from which men have by definition been excluded." They were all naked, naturally, as the book had promised. I looked from one to the other in the clearing, noting the differences more than the similarities, initially, until the similarities began to dominate the differences and, to my surprise, I found myself gradually growing bored. "But I am different," said one. "So am I," said another, in a somewhat different, slightly lower tone. "Truly different," she added. "I'm afraid I am not," I confessed. "That must be why you have come among us," said still another, with a smile I could not fully understand, while those in the distance, those who perhaps could no more hear than be heard, raised their spears in unison and beat their butts against the unrelenting ground.

The Dinosaur in the Living Room

It stands there, the dinosaur in the living room, with its long neck arced above the writing table. This is its armor, these oval plaques, each with its sharp point that hurts no one. This is its backbone, its spine in an otherwise spineless world. Flesh and bone, form and content – who could separate them? Carnivorous? In no way. Vegetarian? Not at all. It lives on light, on an interior illumination that nevertheless has its origins outside, with one foot in the dirt, and in the dirt a suggestion of water. What is astonishing is the weight of the beast, the weight of a life, for it is nothing less. To bear such a burden, and in such a small place, much too small for such a being, crutches have been given to the creature, but not of humankind, rising from the ground, but the most slender of airy supports, themselves practically invisible, descending from above, and so the beast arches over us, indifferent to what we do, even as we write, reminding us that what we do to right the wrongs of this world we do not only in its company but in its shadow as well.

Country of Bridges

Ours is the country of bridges. That is how we are known, both at home and abroad, among the ignorant and the scholarly alike. Even in our founding myth, we are nothing but water. The tears of God, so runs the story, though tears of grief, or joy, or grief and joy, remains to this day a matter of dispute both among the scholars and the ignorant. God cried, and the earth was flooded, so the story would have it; and God continues to cry, at least in the story; and thus not only the fact but the necessity of bridges in our country. Bridges when we speak as well as when we listen, bridges when we look each at the other, bridges when we touch, even the fragrance of a flower is said to be a bridge in the language of our country, as is language itself. For some, in fact, in the country of bridges everything is a bridge, everything must be a bridge. And yet others, and with an equal conviction if not an equal composure, claim that if everything is bridge, nothing is, and in their certainty point to the land, to the earth itself, the little that is left, and more than point, stamp their feet and refuse to take a single step beyond.

Sign and Signature

Two men, sitting on the curb, are enjoying a rare literary discussion over a bottle of white wine and a loaf of dark bread. "Only poetry can express the reality in which thought and feeling can find their marriage in the world today," says the slimmer, more elegant of the two, "difficult as that marriage must be." "That is nonsense," says the other, and with equal conviction. "Only prose is capable of giving voice to the details of life in this void." "Ridiculous," says the less robust. "Prose is without measure and therefore incapable of providing exactly that which makes the perception of detail possible, and thus giving difference form." "Haven't you realized," says the more down-to-earth speaker, looking up at his more elegant companion, "that our time is itself without measure and that therefore paradoxical as it may sound only a form without measure can provide a suggestion of measure by calling into question the very idea of form?" The more the two men speak, the more they disagree, until one draws a switchblade from his pocket and attacks the other, then disappears in silence into the crowd. But who has won the argument, the authorities ask, searching for the survivor, as if the mere fact of survival could be read as a sign of victory, in this case, rather than of loss, and not as proof of the crime itself.

In the Darkness of the Church

A young man stood in the darkness of the church, not far from the gigantic portals of the entrance, regarding from the shadows the believers who, one by one, stopped at the baptismal font to fondle the water before touching their forehead with a moistened finger and then kneeling to the altar, as if in the darkness he himself were preparing to pounce on the frailest of the worshippers. And they all looked frail, elderly widows in mourning for their lives, an old man stuttering upon a cane, even the speechless young woman as much afraid of life, it seemed, as desirous of it. The young man watched them from the shadows disappear into the pews and the church appeared to grow somehow more deserted and more desolate with each additional solitary individual. Unable to bear the observation of the young man any longer the old man threw himself onto a floor stone and began to kiss what remained of the outline of the visor of a holy warrior. "How dare you desecrate the church in such a manner?" the young man cried out from his place in the darkness, only in a whisper, as he lifted the other back onto his feet with one hand and, with the other, thrust the cane back into his hand. "In what manner would you prefer?" the old man cried back, straightening himself, although with difficulty. "Mine is no kiss of Judas. I only come to praise the work and worth of each and every footstep in this place."

Enlightenment

A man sits at his desk at night, writing. The painted room in which he works, his study, is aflood in light. But what is striking is the reach of shadow poised to overwhelm the person at the desk, as if only the act of writing could keep the darkness at bay. The darkness itself would not be visible were it not for the reading lamp upon the desk, would not be visible, in other words, as darkness were it not for the desire for enlightenment that has brought the person to light the lamp in the first place. Where does the oil in the lamp come from? How many deaths made possible this light? How many forests fell to make these walls? And even if it is only an image in a work of art we are looking at, what are we to make of the reach and range of such enlightenment? Where does the illumination end? And the darkness, our darkness, real as it is, real as it has to be, how can it survive the light?

The Arrival of the Message

The message is for you. But old as you are now, old as the messenger is, bald and short of breath, the once strong back bowed, the face lined, the uniform frayed and discolored and torn in places, it is clear that the message has taken more time to arrive than anyone had imagined and that under the circumstances it is not possible to know with certainty if the message is still valid, if the emperor is still alive, or if the empire, such as it is, or was, can be said now even to exist.

The Absconditen

At the creation of the universe God appeared to make His one and only mistake, so say the Absconditen, and in the Big Bang the Author of all things blew Himself up: thus the world as it is, even to this day, thus the world as it will be, to the end of time. Among the Absconditen, however, the disappearance of God from the story is said to be no reason for despair; on the contrary, it is claimed to be the necessary and indeed the only ground for human freedom, and thus the apparent mistake is no mistake at all; for at the moment of the creation the Godhead was multiplied into each and every being in the universe, from the beginning to the end of time, and thus even into those who refuse to believe, and who, so say the Absconditen, by the force of their refusal make belief as belief possible.

Cassandra

Cassandra, the most beautiful of Troy's daughters, is the first to see the body of her brother, mutilated, beyond the walls of the city, the first to mourn the fall of the king her father, the first, too, to lament the fate of her sisters and her mother. Nothing is said of her prophetic powers, not in the earliest reports, at any rate, nothing apparently needs to be said. It is we who know the final story and not she, we who remember how Ajax, that bulwark of a man, would ravish her in front of the altar where she prayed for wisdom, and how the leader of the army, great Agamemnon himself, would rescue her – if rescue is the word – only to be murdered, with her, by his wife. It is the later legends that ascribe to her the gift of prophecy, and through Apollo, who is said to have bestowed on the woman prophetic powers only to win her for himself – so runs the story; and, when he failed, and loveless once again, added a further gift which turned the apparent blessing into a curse by causing her, the prophetess, never to be believed by anyone who heard her prophecy. And so it is, today, when she cries out to us, here, where we are, now, at the office, cries out the death of love, of honor, of belief, of feeling, truth, and innocence at once, we, who know the ancient story, we for whom the catastrophe has already happened, shut our ears and turn back to our work.

Black Fruit

The black fruit hangs from the lowest branch of the tallest tree. More than one tree, too. From each and every tree. Words, words, you say. I will not look, and if I do not look I will not listen. I refuse to look. I refuse to listen. But it is impossible not to look, impossible not to listen. You are not blind. You have ears, after all. You will have to move, at some point in time you will have to move. But how can you move if you do not look to see where to put your foot? Stay where you are, stay here, forever? It is not possible. Open your eyes, then. It is winter. Everything has gone black, everything has been burnt. The trees themselves, though they still stand, scorched as they are, continue smoking. Letters, you say, looking at the desolation of the landscape. The letters of the alphabet, and more than the alphabet, the silence itself, in each and every word, at least for those who can still read.

The Wild Dogs of Parnassos

Unknown to anyone you have climbed Mt. Parnassos. How wonderful, you say, to be here now! How wonderful to look into the blue, the empty sky! How wonderful to breathe the clear iambic air, even if you have a bit of trouble with the footing now. But at your age would it not be better to lower your sights a little and to observe what is around you? That is when you see the other mountain. There are two peaks to Mt. Parnassos, it turns out, not one. How could the books have failed to mention this? Have you climbed the right summit, you ask yourself. Should you not, to be sure, climb the other as well? Then you discover the enormous dog standing in the gap between the peaks looking menacingly up at you upon your rocky pedestal. You have read about the wild dogs of Parnassos, escaped from their bucolic idyll herding local sheep, ready now to pounce on any living creature. Under the circumstances would it not be wiser, you ask yourself, not to climb the alternative Parnassos but simply to go home as fast as possible? Only then do you realize that if you can no longer ascend the other summit because of the dog, for the same reason you can not descend this one.

Human to Hero

There sits Orestes, the avenger, waiting to be called. There is Cassandra, silent now, a foreigner even when at home, and her brother next to her on the bench, the one whose thoughts even now run about in circles. There is Achilles, on the other side, not yet angry, or no longer so. And Agamemnon, walking back and forth, hand in hand with his wife, a still beautiful woman who has only begun to think of the deed of many consequences, yet seems ravaged if not ravished by the mere possibility. The Furies are there, too, still furious, but uncertain now against whom to direct their mayhem. As head of personnel you have no choice but to watch them on the other side of the glass as you look listlessly at the list of job skills on your desk. But what can be done with heroes in an age such as our own? There is no work for the likes of such characters today. And perhaps it is better so, you think, if they simply go back to the human community from which they have come.

Watchtowers

I have a castle in the country that I wish to keep, a little keepsake, once a royal keep, the massive dreary walls refurbished now, as far as paint can remove the blood stains and the pain of other people, and what I like most, cold as it is, and always will be here, inadequate as the heating system is, inadequate as any form of fire could ever be to warm these dreadful walls, short of absolute conflagration, is to step outside and pace the parapets, in foul weather and fair, and from my castle to observe the other towers in the distance, as far as the eye can see, in forest and in field, where people like myself, keepers of the ancient keeps, keep watch as well from what remains of the storied ancestral properties, even if nothing more than a single stone, now, the earth beneath your feet.

A Final Flowering

Soldiers are what we are, what we were, and what we have been for a millennium, a millennium if not more, coming out of unrecorded time, descending from the North after ascending from the South, to pillage and to plunder, to mix and marry, proud of our exploits, our conquests. We were there with Malcolm at Birnham Wood, we were there with the Conqueror, and later in the forts and keeps and castles we received for work well done we were there against the English when they invaded what was now our country and still later in the Holy Land there we were again but with the English now against the Infidels, and later still, deprived of our lands and loyalties, there we were when we were needed, and, still later, with the Founding Fathers, too, and in the Civil War, and on both sides of the Great Divide, and beyond, fierce men of war, not to speak of the women, a furious family, as fierce as I am now a man of peace, as furiously opposed to the slaughter as my forefathers were devoted to it. And tonight it is I and I alone among the fallen foliage who lift a glass of oak-aged Scotch to the glow of embers late at night and toast the castles that remain throughout the centuries, the fabulous, familiar, indestructible castles of the air: dark pebble seed of origins, starry tree of a final flowering.

Salad Days

In the Round

A monstrance is the receptacle in which the consecrated Host is exposed for adoration. It shows, or demonstrates, the truth, or what some people claim to be the truth, even the truth of truth. It is thus, in its own way, a kind of warning, a sign of what without it would not be the truth, the whole truth, and nothing but the truth, and thus the lack, in truth, of truth itself. It is a portent of something otherwise not clear, something that deviates from the normal and is thus abnormal, even monstrous in and of itself. It does not pass muster, in other words, though for that very reason, it may surpass the conventional or assembled wisdom of the masses at any given moment and thus frighten, even terrify, those for whom the normal constitutes the norm. At least so remonstrate those who oppose the conventional in their own eyes. We who are not priests, we who consider ourselves the hosts and ghosts and even guests of other words, we who have seen the demon in the demonstration, time and again, can only acknowledge what we have seen, in fear and trembling, among the monstrous possibilities. Monsters ourselves, at least in the eyes of those who oppose us, we can do nothing with the object at hand but to acknowledge it, in all its history, its difference, even from itself, its etymology, so to speak, in time. Make it a word, in other words, and pass it round.

The Liberation Parade

Gunshots exploded in the distance. The gunshots did not trouble us, for better or for worse, we had grown used to such sounds. "After all," Betty Jane was saying, "when all is said and done, sex is a weapon." "I could not agree with you more," J. B. answered, pivoting like the turret of a tank and focusing in turn on each and every woman in the room. You could see the wounded walking by the window. The walking wounded, that was what the authorities called them. Then came the wheelchairs. After the wheelchairs came the coffin, borne on the shoulders of our local elect, our councilmen and women. Each person formed part of a unit, each unit was repeated in the same order, walking wounded, wheelchairs, coffin, each unit preceded by a healthy child, boy or girl, in alternation, each child bearing a sign on which could be read if not the name of a country the name of a war. The Liberation Parade, that is what the event had come to be called, and I had the clear and distinct impression, listening to Betty Jane and J. B. exchanging words, that they were not aware of what was happening outside, or, if aware, thought what was happening in the world of no significance whatsoever.

In the Woods

Something has gone wrong, we are sure of it, as sure as we can be, we have informed the authorities, as the authorities have requested, time and again, when something goes wrong, but the authorities have done nothing to help us, once again, at least as far as we can see. An old lady alone in a house out in the woods. What does she do out there, we want to know. Where does she get her money? A small house, true, we admit, but a house nevertheless. And then the child, her grandchild, so she says, the one that visits her with that red riding hood – too red, we said. How could a child come into the money for a hood like that? And why that color, red, so out of place, so out of character for someone raised the way that she was raised: strict and straight and straight ahead. And the wine! What kind of mother would send her child out into the world – into the woods! – with nothing more substantial than a bottle of wine? And, for that matter, what kind of grandmother would spend her days in bed, day after day, waiting for her bottle? A bottle to be brought her by a child! Something is not in order here, we said. Do not be fooled by those commands to walk the straight and narrow path. What's wrong with flowers, we said, what's wrong with birds, the songs of birds – what kind of parent would forbid her child to listen to the birds or make a bouquet of the flowers? So what if you must leave the given path? You can come back to it. Something is out of order here. And then the men, wolves, really! What could they all be doing in that house, small as it is. Ambitious men, we said, men with a lean and hungry look – not the kind of man we know in our part of the woods, and certainly not the kind of man you might bring home for your mother, or your daughter, not to mention your grandmother, bed-ridden though she be. They come but they never leave, those men. What could have happened in that house, we ask ourselves. What do they do all night together? Why does a woman far advanced in years remain in bed all day, day after day, a blanket drawn up to her snout, eyeing us suspiciously, as if we her neighbors were the ones guilty of something, as if looking through a window were itself a crime?

Rapunzel

"Rapunzel, Rapunzel, let down your hair," cries a young man, barely more than a boy, but in a voice so low no one can hear, as if he were crying out not to another human being but to the light itself to fall at his feet. How can I or anyone else actually speak like this, he thinks. If anyone or anything is to be let down, I am going to be the one. For everyone knows that the castle has long been in ruins, there is no woman in the window, there can be no woman in the window for the simple reason that there is no window, only this wall as thick as air, and you are only one more person in need of companionship. Perhaps I should have paid no attention to the stories I was told as a child, perhaps it is they that have brought you here, he tells himself, where you are now, crying out in a voice hardly your own and for nothing more substantial in the darkness than a ladder of light.

Fairy Tale

Once upon a time, there was a young woman who was in the habit late in the day of strolling to a fountain at the edge of her parents' estate. There she would sit on the stone ledge of the fountain and toss a golden ring into the air, then catch it before it could fall to the earth. One day, more bored than usual, for it was not so easy in that day and age to be rich and beautiful and not be bored, she threw the ring even higher into the air than usual and lost it in the light, so that it fell through her fingers, and not into the dirt, as she had feared, but into the fountain, where it glittered for a moment before it disappeared into the depths. Not to be thwarted in her game, she rolled up her sleeves and plunged her hands into the water to search the depths for what she had lost, but found to her dismay that there was no bottom to the water, at least none that she could touch, and she began to cry. A frog heard her – at least so she would say at home – and asked her in a deep but not unpleasant voice: "Why are you crying, my dear girl?" "I am not a girl," she said, sharply, for she would speak to a frog in no other voice, not even if the frog were a prince in disguise. "I am a woman, and a rich one at that. But I have lost my ring in that fountain, and every attempt I have made to find it has only muddied the waters." "What would you give me if I brought it back?" asked the frog, apparently used to such transactions. "Pearls, or gold," said the woman. "Whatever you want." "What would a frog do with pearls or gold," said the frog, "or even a job in your father's company?" "What would you like, then?" said the woman, apparently no stranger to commercial actions herself. "To share your table and your bed," said the frog at once. "As you wish," said the woman, who by this time had convinced herself that she loved the ring more than anything else in the world and would do anything to get it back. The frog disappeared into the water and returned with the ring, which the woman took from his tongue without a word and hurried home to her parents.

It was not until the next day and at dinner that there was a knock on the front door. It was the frog. It was a rather ugly frog. At least that was the opinion of the father, though the mother said that she had seen worse. But being the kind of parents who believe in the importance of table talk the father asked his daughter why she had turned suddenly pale. "Because of a promise I made," she said and explained what had happened at the fountain the previous day. "You must keep your word," the father said, sternly, "and all the more so if your frog is no prince."

Alternative Ending

It was not until the next day and at dinner that there was a knock on the front door. It was the frog. It was a rather ugly frog. At least that was the opinion of the father, though the mother said that she had seen worse. But being the kind of parents who believe in the importance of table talk the father asked his daughter why she had turned suddenly pale. "Because of a promise I made," she said and explained what had happened at the fountain the previous day.

"A woman who does not keep her word is not for me," said the frog, and on these words turned into a prince of a man, and strode once and forever out of the house.

No Laughing Matter

"You have made my daughter laugh," said the king, "something no one has ever been able to do, not even I myself, and for that reason, I am going to overlook the charges that have been brought against you, grave as they are, and to give her to you in marriage." "But she laughed *at* me," said the young man, "even as I tried to maintain my innocence." "A laugh is a laugh," said the father, "and if you continue to be ridiculous, especially in your own defense, I am sure you will live happily ever after."

Letter to the Authorities

It has recently been brought to my attention that one of our residents has been the object of complaints, complaints which, even if unfounded, might appear in a light not altogether favorable to us. "Snow White," people cry out, as if to mock the woman with a name that is clearly not her own. We who have seen snow black, we who have seen snow grey, we who have seen the corpses of the winter tossed aside on our roads at the end of a season to make way for another ask ourselves why so much attention should be paid to a color, even if only in mockery. In my previous reports I have had no choice nevertheless but to point out that the woman in question was raised among men she considers dwarfs. This I consider the chief factor in the formation of her character as well as in her attitude toward the male sex in general. The vertically challenged, I should add, have a bad reputation among us; they have traditionally been associated with the mines, here, and with the usual reservations toward darkness and dirt; and while these particular creatures – and I should point out that there was not a single female among them until the young lady was taken in – would seem to have insisted upon the proprieties, and in particular upon cleanliness, they left her alone, abandoned to her own devices, and without proper schooling, day after day, while they went off to work in the mines to make a living. Thus she grew up in something like absolute isolation, interrupted though it was by its very opposite, once the men had come home from work. I should add that in both cases, alone and in the company of the men, she was expected to perform the household chores; that was, in fact, the very raison d'être for her existence there. These tasks ranged from bed-making to bread-making, from cooking and washing to sewing and ironing, in short, doing whatever was necessary to keep seven men, as the only female present, comfortable and in good health and spirits. Nothing less than perfection was expected of her, an ideal impossible to attain, needless to say, and her character, so I would maintain, can not be understood, can not even be approached, without the sense of failure that inevitably accompanies such an ideal. But she performed her tasks to her employers' complete satisfaction, as is stated in the letter of reference forwarded to us, even though it should be mentioned that she received nothing more substantial for her efforts than room and board.

It is true that the so-called dwarfs looked after her, in their own way, and provided her with warnings and advice as well as room and board, but as they were at work all day it was not possible for them to supervise either her behavior when alone or her visitors when she had visits. Thus it was possible for a woman who later claimed to be her step-mother to talk her way into the house, and not just once but three times, and, in each case, having won the young woman's confidence, to poison her: first, disguised as a merchant, with a poisoned blouse; then, disguised as a travelling beautician, with a poisoned comb; and, finally, disguised as a peasant, with a poisoned apple, half of which – the unpoisoned half – she ate herself in the presence of the young woman as a token of sincerity. The first two times the seven men were able to revive the young woman, but not the third, though they resorted to all the means at their disposal; and, giving her up for dead, but unwilling to bury her once and forever in the earth – their element, I should add – enclosed her in a glass box.

Thus it was that a man who happened to be passing by at that very moment saw her. It was love at first sight, at least on his side, and being himself not only a prince but a man of means he offered a tidy sum for the woman's body. The seven refused on principle. More, they felt insulted, and to a man, and were about to send him off with as good a beating as they could muster when he fell to his knees in front of them and confessed his love for a woman he did not and could not know and with whom any form of communication was impossible. So impressive was his passion that the seven, without another word, gave up the woman who had served them so well.

The rest of the story I need not relate – the details are known to all, even to the point of contradiction. Suffice it to say that the young man's colleagues, for he had not come alone, hoisted the coffin on to their shoulders at his command and set off on their long and homeward journey. They had hardly left the country when one of the men stumbled on a root, and this slight alteration in the rhythm of things was enough to dislodge the apple from the young woman's throat – a vulgarian would say that the lady burped – and, free of the apple at last, she woke to the world.

What might have appeared as a form of rescue once upon a time must have struck the young woman in question as a kind of kidnapping, and by relative giants, and thus it should come as no surprise if at the first available opportunity she sought refuge among us. She refuses to confirm or deny the story related here, and goes about her daily tasks admirably, indifferent to the past and focused only on the work at hand. In this regard she can be considered the ideal patient. Nothing seems to discourage her, not even the name-calling to which she has been subjected. I need not point out the ignorance of those who have made claims against her. There are no princes today, even the title was abolished hundreds of years ago, at the founding of our nation, and the characterization of the step-mother, as far as I am concerned – and I am not alone – invalidates the entire story.

Beautiful People

They arrived in the dead of winter, a man and a woman, and spoke with no one in the town. Beautiful people, we said, if we said anything. What can they want here? What has a town like ours for the likes of them? Soon spring was sprung and sprang into the trees and meadows. The rivers ran again; the wild boars ranted. The birds stitched and un-stitched the sky, as usual, day after day, sunrise and sunset. And still, they spoke with no one. Beautiful people, we said, but with the budding of contempt. Then summer came and with the summer drought. The rivers dwindled to a whisper and then disappeared. The crops refused to grow, even the grasses lost their colors. We went about our work with furrows in our faces. Only they remained the same. Beautiful people, we said, not without scorn. Autumn came, and winter followed, only they remained the same. Immortals, someone scoffed. As if youth had no end. As if the gods themselves did not grow old. Immortal promises, we cried, immortal lies!

The Modern Couple

Hänsel, not Hansel. That is what we were told, and in a tone that annoyed us, as if we were incapable of pronouncing a single word correctly on our own. Hänsel and Gretel. Brother and Sister. So they said, standing hand in hand before us, with their picturebook smiles. We knew the story, those of us who still read. We knew where they were coming from. The airs those two put on, that's what we said, coming from where they came. How could they think we would believe that story? Imagine – a mother who would send her children out into the woods just to get rid of them. And a witch in a gingerbread house! That is not a witch, we said, that is a cliché, a view of woman we refuse to countenance in this day and age. And then the hunger – to eat your own house down! She the window, he the roof. Typical, we said: women and windows, men and roofs. The long perspectives and the act of closure, the bright translucent and the dull opaque – all that to be consumed, destroyed, subverted! And for what? The modern couple? Hänsel and Gretel? Not on your life!

Night after Night

Night after night at Aladdin's Lamp a male voice can be heard, crying: "And now, from Cairo, Egypt, Badiah Awad!" And a small Jewish woman from Brooklyn, New York, clad only in a coin girdle and bra she has sewn herself, mounts the stage and under a veil blue as the sky at night makes the coins tremble like stars to the music of an alien band. Not a few people would like to live in a world in which professionally speaking gender does not matter, and yet it is as clear as the stars when the stars are clear that this is a fiction in which a man and a woman can not change roles. For the dancer is a woman in the night, and the men are looking in the darkness for something they do not and apparently can not find in their own lives. So the music resounds, the circles of the drinks accumulate on the table, the coins tremble like stars, the veil conceals and reveals what at the same time must be revealed and concealed, and love's treasury – whatever worth the currency – hangs by a thread that, for the moment at least, no one cuts.

The Absence of the Father

In our country family life has traditionally been built around the absence of the father. This can be seen in the furniture, arranged in family groups, in which the father is rarely to be found, at least not on work days, and never in the natural light. In the absence of the father, it has become the custom of the family to talk about the importance of the presence of the father. In this way, a myth has been established in which the more the father absents himself the more the father becomes the central figure of the myth. As the centrality of his presence is based on its absence, only the father's actual presence can call into question his authority. And thus it becomes more and more necessary for the father to absent himself. Nothing is allowed to interfere with this story-telling, and opposition to the myth is considered its ultimate confirmation.

At Any Moment

He leaves his wife where she has fallen on the gravel in the moonlight before the house and drives away. Where he goes no one knows. Tomorrow she will not be there, no more than the moonlight: that much is clear. She hears the dog bark, feels the rough animal tongue on her cheek, rises to remembered light, and makes her battered way inside the house. Tomorrow nothing will be like this, tomorrow she will lie in bed, her bruises to herself, and when the children come home from school they will speak as they always have spoken, and life will be as it is, as it always has been, as if nothing had happened, or could happen, and at any moment.

Four Hooves

I

She took the head in her hands, then hit it against the wall, but the boy did not react, she had lost the ability to make him react, slam the head as she would, there was only the wall, a white wall, and even it would not be there, behind the head, had he not stood, the boy, no doubt out of politeness, polite as he was, when she entered the room, so that the wall was there, had he not stood they might have spoken, this one who refused, polite as he was, even to cry out, even to protest.

II

But even the silence, loud as it was, could not efface the sounds on the other side of the wall, sounds there was no escaping in the house, such as it was, the walls not what walls had once been, in childhood, at least her childhood, the sounds of music, music that was always there, no doubt it was against the sounds, the music, if music it was, sounds that had called her to the room and left her speechless, that she had to act, the head in her hands.

III

It was by the ears, in point of fact, that the head was slammed against the wall, the head of the one who would not cry out, would not protest, the one who in the sounds refused even to speak, and thus not speaking, not protesting, not even crying out, could not efface the sounds, the silences.

IV

From the other side of the wall, the other sounds could be heard, the sounds that had been hers, at least for a moment, the sounds of the horse, out of the sounds the image of the horse appeared, the white horse, sounds of water and ice, like mountain rocks, sounds that could carry a person away, darkness, the white horse, the cool water, drink, the four hooves.

Black Holes

Fifty years have passed since he tried to kill you, yet there he is still, he or someone like him, a child on either side, a boy and a girl, smiling. What do they think of their father now, you wonder, looking at the photograph, what do they think of their mother, in all likelihood the one who took the picture you are looking at, so young then, the one who married him and stayed with him, through everything, if indeed she did, dead as they must be now, the smiling children in their Sunday best, the father in his sheet and pointed hood, an arm around each smiling child, equally, only the eyes visible, and visible only as black holes. What do they think, what should they think of this time that has survived its principles, its laws and customs, even as others lived and died for them? What should they think of you, for that matter, looking at the photograph in the museum of memories, remembering the march, the policemen with their guns, the dogs, the beatings, the electric shocks, the jail, the sweatbox in the courtyard of the jail, the man with his skull cracked open, holding his life in his hands, looking at it all, in triumph?

One Or the Other

I do not know how to begin, since you are not listening, so what is the point of talking, you will not listen, or if you listen it will only be to put the words behind you, for the silence, you will say, as if the silence could ever be the same, now, after all that has been said, said and not said. You see how I have to begin, as if there were no beginning, as if I had to explain even what I mean when I say that I do not know how to begin because it is language that has broken down between us and that is why even this I cannot communicate. Words, you will say, that is all that is left, words and silences, and if you say I am exaggerating I can only answer that I have to exaggerate to make you see, even if you say you will never see what I am saying if I exaggerate. Nothing happened. It meant nothing. That is what you will say. Only look into my eyes. You no longer resemble yourself. Not in my eyes. Or the idea I had of you. In your eyes. You had to smash the idea to be real. It was the idea that was at fault. It was the idea that had to be broken and so you broke it. You wanted me to look at you and see you as you are. But when I looked I saw a person who had fallen out of all resemblance and dragged me down, too. And did you lift me up? Did you think of me at all after I had fallen if fallen I really had? I thought of you all the time, I could not forget, each time I looked into your eyes, how you had fallen. I wanted to lift you out of what I saw, but every time I spoke I plunged you further into it and myself as well. You will say I am being hysterical, the more I talk of what has happened the more you say I am being hysterical, and if I am not hysterical I soon will be. I won't deny it. You who caused the pain are the only person who can absolve me of it and all you can say is that you are contemptuous of that type of pain. I am making something out of nothing. It is all my doing. I can read that in your eyes, it is all my fault, I will never understand you, I would have to be unfaithful to understand you and if I were unfaithful I would be unworthy. Now you will have to go through life seeking your likeness in another and your likeness will have to be unfaithful. One or the other!

A Familiar Act

1

He is not going to have a woman here for the night, says the father. Why not, the daughter asks. Because of the example, it would set for all you girls. We are not girls, says the daughter, we are women, and as for the example it would set it would be one of tolerance appropriate for an open and democratic society such as our own. I do not believe that ours is an open and democratic society, says the father. One day in the future history will arrive at such a society and abolish itself, but until that day arrives I am the one who makes the rules here.

2

So that is what you look like, says the mother, in the bedroom of her son, gazing at the naked body of the girlfriend. My son is a lucky boy. But you cannot go out into the living room, not even once you have put on your clothes, not with my husband there. My husband has his principles, as you know. He cannot bring a woman home. That is the way it is. That is the way it has to be. You must accept us as we are. But do not despair. The situation is not as tragic as it looks. You can always use the window. In this house there is always a window – if only you know how to open it.

3

What are you doing, says the father, looking into the bedroom and finding all the others at the desk before the window. What does it look like we are doing, says the mother. We are engaged in a familiar act. They are trying to get out of here, in accordance with your rules and principles, which no one here would ever think of calling into question, and certainly not when you happen to be present, rare as those times now are, and I as a mother am helping them. So are the girls. When I want to get out of the house, says the father, and that is every day, I use the front door.

An Exemplary Figure

From A to B objects have been moved. There is no problem here, all agree on the fact. Only our president has no knowledge of this movement, some say, and thus is ignorant, if not innocent, and this is the problem, others claim, for if our leader has no knowledge he is obviously not our leader, and if he has knowledge he is obviously responsible for the movement and thus not ignorant, not innocent, for this is a movement that should not have occurred, it is said, the president himself has forbidden this movement, and by official decree, thus for the president to have initiated the movement, and by official decree, would amount to violating by decree his own decree, an impossible situation, and yet all agree on the fact, from A to B objects have been moved, that is the problem. Why not tell the truth? That is what the president tells us to do. If he tells the truth, he will become an exemplary figure, his own model, and yet if he is ignorant, and of the truth, how can he tell it, and if he is guilty of violating his own decree – and his decree is our law – then he cannot be expected to turn a finger toward his own office, not with the law as it is, and thus he cannot be expected to tell the truth, and without the truth he cannot be an exemplary figure. There is really no solution to the problem and since there is no solution, for the president at least, there is ultimately no problem.

The Consolations of Mortality

Vulcan, the blacksmith, a man of volcanic temperament, outraged by his wife's behavior, forges a chain of metal so fine that nothing of the links can be seen, only what can be caught in them, a chain as refined as the air itself, and placing it around the bed of his wife catches the woman and her lover, Mars, in the invisible threads, then calls in the gods to witness the shame. But is that not shameful for everyone, say the children, a boy and a girl, as their father points out the details of the painting in front of them. That may have been the case, once upon a time, replies the father, but that was a different time, and then to change the subject adds what a good thing it is, and for all concerned, that their mother is no Venus.

In the Mountains

We had been walking in the mountains for some time and stood together now on the summit looking out into the distance, only in the distance there was nothing to be seen, nothing but a sea of mist out of which occasional peaks appeared to rise like words or islands in a vast and far-flung archipelago before disappearing once again into the silence. I saw then that each of us had cast a shadow on the blank, but that around my shadow there shone a rainbow ring. I could not for one moment believe that I alone bore such a rainbow, that I alone glowed with such light. "And how is it with you?" I cried out. "Do you, too, have a rainbow round your shoulders? Are we others in shadow and you alone in the light?"

Voices

I

"You can't object to what has happened."
"Why not?"
"Because nothing has happened!"

II

"Now you know how people react who have broken their principles."
"I have not broken my principles. I have simply changed them."
"That is precisely how people react who have broken their principles."

III

"You have no rights."
"That's fascism."
"That's reality."

IV

"If anything like this ever happens again, I'm not going to tell anyone."
"So I am already part of a series, the diminishing end of an infinite regression. And you are committed to lying."
"I am committed to nothing."

Pleasant Dreams

I

"Why did you marry me?"
"Because you are different from the others."
"I'm not."
"Don't say that."
"Or if I am everyone is."
"Even if it's true don't say that."

II

"Have you thought of working?"
"Work is for other people."
"Someone has to make the money."
"You do that very well."
"And the chores?"
"I can't cook. I won't shop. And I hate cleaning."
"So do I."
"But you do it."
"It has to get done."

III

"I don't believe you love me."
"I more than love you. I worship you. Isn't that enough?"
"It's too much."
"What do you want?"
"An ordinary life."
"I refuse to be ordinary."

"How do you expect to live?"
"You'll look after me."
"And if I don't?"
"Someone else will."

Near and Far

"Sex is a meeting place," I cries out, proud to have found a formula at last that could be proclaimed by any person, young or old, in public or in private, in silence or aloud, regardless of race, religion, color, nationality, even of sex itself. "A meeting place," I repeats, proudly, to the apartment walls and beyond the walls to the lines of the street. I says it often. I says it to the trees in their protective cages, I says it to the office buildings rising out of the concrete, I says it to the birds between the buildings, I says it to the garbage in the streets, and to the people searching in the garbage for something of sustenance. I says it to the moon, the melancholy, marble moon, even to the stars themselves.

Traffic Lights

1

The traffic lights turn red.

The taxi cab comes to a stop. The passenger in the back seat goes on talking, but the driver pays no attention to what he is saying. She is looking at the light.

The next thing she knows is that her head is being banged against the dashboard of the car. She turns her attention to the left, as best she can under the circumstances, and sees that it is a strange man, outside, in the street, who has reached his hand into her space, grabbed her by the hair, and is now banging her head against the dashboard.

"Why are you banging my head against the dashboard?" she asks, as clearly as she can under the circumstances.

"Because a woman should not be driving a cab."

"What should a woman be doing?"

"Staying home and having babies!"

The light turns green, the man releases her hair and gets back into the car behind hers, and then both drive off with the traffic.

2

"Welcome home," says the mother, putting a drink into the young woman's hands.

"How is the choreography going?" asks the father, sipping a martini of his own.

"I'm working on a piece based on the rhythm of traffic lights," the daughter answers, sitting down in a set of easy chairs that reproduce someone else's idea of the family group.

"Traffic lights," the father says. "How do the dancers come in?"

"That's what I'm working on."

"You should never have left the New York City Ballet," the mother says.

Then she looks at her daughter more carefully.

"Why is only your left arm tanned and not your right?"

"Because when I sit on the roof garden," the daughter answers quickly, much too quickly, the mother thinks, "that's where the sun comes from."

"I didn't know you had a roof garden," says the father.

"She doesn't have a roof garden," says the mother. "There is no roof garden in her building. Can't you see that she has a job in New York City driving a cab?"

3

The mother begins to cry.

"My daughter is not a cab driver," she sobs. "That is not what I raised my girl to be."

"She's my girl, too," says the father.

"Do you want our daughter to be a cab driver?"

"She wants to be an independent woman."

"Then give her enough money to be one."

A Very Funny Story

"Lift your end up," the husband tells the wife, and she lifts up her end as he does his, and then together they strap the canoe into place on the car roof.

Through the window of their next-door-neighbor's kitchen they can see their neighbor watching them.

"Better late than never," says the husband, as Junior runs out to the car and begins to play the drums on the brand-new silver canoe.

Then comes his wife's mother, inching forward in her walking cage, its silver glints turning her own complexion green.

"And to think that this is where the great man camped," says the father, once they have arrived across the water, hauling out his copy of the book.

"How can you know that?" asks his wife.

"I read it," he says, and pats the book.

The next day the father, the mother and the child go fishing.

Grandmother they put in the folding chair facing the wide waste of water.

"Don't worry about me," Grandmother says.

They do not. Each day they go out fishing in the new canoe, each day they come back and find Grandmother folded up in the reading chair.

On the last day of their holiday they decide to go fishing one last day.

When they come back Grandmother is once again folded up in the folding chair.

Father and son prepare the trout while the mother lies down for a last nap.

When she awakes her mother is still asleep in the folding chair.

"She must be dead," Junior says.

"Wishful thinking," his mother replies.

Her husband gives the old woman a nudge.

"It's not wishful thinking," he says.

"What are we going to do now?" asks the mother.

"We're going to do what we always do at the end of a holiday," says the father. "We're going to go home."

"What about Grandma?"

"We'll have to put her in the canoe."

So they put Grandma in the canoe, pack up their tent and supplies, and then paddle back to the town where they have left their car.

The father goes into the local bar and asks for a telephone book, only to discover that there is no entry under Undertakers.

"We'll have to take her home," he says.

So they put the canoe on top of the car, with Grandma in it, and begin the long drive home.

"Can we stop at the shopping mall?" Junior asks, as they pass the first of what will be many shopping malls.

"I hate shopping malls," says the mother.

"Of course, we can," says the father.

"They're ruining the country," says the mother.

"As you know it," adds the father.

They stop, and Junior buys a plastic gun.

As they are about to enter the car the father realizes that there is nothing above it.

"Somebody has stolen the lousy canoe!" the mother cries out.

"Don't blame me," the father answers. "It's not my mother."

Junior points his gun at his parents and makes a series of explosive sounds.

"We'll have to buy another one," the father says.

"And Grandma? Have you thought about Grandma?"

"Of course, I have," says the father. "I was always the one who had to think about her."

Statements

1

I woke up naked strapped to a bed in a white room. The room was very cold. It had three solid walls and the fourth wall consisted of metal bars separating it from a larger room. I am not sure how long I remained strapped to the bed, but after some time I was transferred to a chair where I was kept shackled by my hands and feet for what must have been two to three weeks and allowed to get up only to go to the toilet, which consisted of a bucket in a corner of the room. Loud music was constantly played and repeated every fifteen minutes interrupted only by a hiss or a crackling noise. The guards wore masks to conceal their faces. At certain intervals I was given lectures and made to understand that I was an enemy of the values I would have to be taught, even though I had shown myself incapable of understanding anything like values, they said, given what I had done, in spite of my insisting that I was guilty of nothing, just bad luck, having done nothing except to be in the wrong place at the wrong time.

2

One day one of my interrogators wrapped a towel around my neck and then the men in masks used it to swing me around and then to smash me against a wall. Afterwards they put me into a black box about four feet by three feet and six feet high for what must have been about one and a half to two hours, though it might have been more. It might have been less, too, but I could not tell because they had taken my watch and my memory was no longer working very well. The box was totally black on the inside as well as on the outside. They put a cloth over the box to cut out the light and restrict the air supply. When I was let out I saw that one of the walls of the room had been covered with plywood sheets while I had been inside the box and from now on it was against this wall that I was thrown using the towel around my neck as a sling. Later I was placed in a smaller box. It was not high enough for me to sit upright so I had to crouch. It was always cold in the room, but when the cover was placed over the box it became hot. The wounds on my leg began to open and bleed. I don't know how long I remained in the box, I must have slept from time to time or maybe I just fainted. Then I was taken out of the box and put on what looked like a hospital bed and strapped down with belts. A black cloth was placed over my face and the interrogators used a mineral water bottle to pour water on the cloth so that I could not breathe. After a few minutes the cloth was removed and the bed was rotated into an upright position so I could vomit. The bed was then lowered back into a horizontal position and the same procedures were carried out with the black cloth and the bottle. Only now water was poured into my mouth, which they forced open, making it difficult for me to say anything.

3

I could see at one point that there was snow on the ground so I knew that the season had changed. Everybody was wearing black now, even the interrogators, they were in masks and army boots and coats and they looked odd and out of place against the snow, they were like words, I thought, but without meaning. They just stood there saying nothing and then the snow was gone but not the masks and the interrogators kept telling me that I was guilty, I had to be guilty, they had my word on that as proof, that was why this had to happen, they had their orders. I was kept naked for about one month without heat in the cell in a standing position with my hands cuffed and shackled above my head and my feet cuffed and shackled to a point in the floor. I fell asleep from time to time and this resulted in all my weight being applied to the handcuffs and both my feet became very swollen and so I tried to lessen the weight by hanging from my wrists alone but this resulted in my wrists becoming even more bruised and swollen than my feet. For interrogation, I was taken to a different room. The sessions lasted for as long as eight hours. If I was thought not to be cooperating I was slapped and punched or smashed against the wall. The beatings were combined with the use of cold water. Some days the cold water was directed at me from a hose by guards while I was still in my cell. Finally, my interrogators poured water down my throat until I thought I was going to drown. They told me I was going to die if I did not make statements. I had made so many statements already that I could not remember what statements I had made. But if they wanted statements I would give them statements, I said, and as many statements as they wanted.

Cheap Contrasts

1

The first requirement was to give up pen and writing pad. Then he was searched for weapons, one man to the left, one man to the right, in the middle a woman with a sub-machine gun, but at a distance, a professional distance, male hands removing from the jacket the following objects and in no order but this: one glasses case (over the heart), one wallet (from the right breast pocket), the camera (from around the neck) and last but not least (from the right side pocket) the miniature tape recorder he had recently purchased from a so-called discount shop at the new shopping mall that had replaced the improvised baseball field of his childhood for what seemed to him a fabulous sum now that it was of absolutely no use.

2

"Remember the rules," said the guide. "And never forget that behind the rules there is a reason for the rules. You may look, but you may not talk. And above all, ask no questions. Except to me, of course. The captives are not allowed to communicate in any way with the outside world, except under our supervision and guidance, of course, and thus only at times known to us in advance and included within the program."

"But you're speaking as if I myself were a prisoner, here," the man without the pen said, looking at the cages in which, instead of animals, men and women had been gathered in groups of four to six.

"Why have you put bags over their heads, and in this heat, in the open air?"

"Disorientation," the guide said.

"But surely they know where they are."

"They know that they are in prison," the guide said. "That is true."

3

The final requirement was to hand over his clothes, except for his underwear, which in fact he was forbidden to remove, and then, on entering the cage, and in accordance with the rules, to turn around and kneel on the burning metal floor. "Now put your head forward," said the guide, in a not unkind and even, possibly, a sympathetic voice, and, as the other obediently inched forward his face, dropped the hood on him.

"You wanted to see what it is like," the guide said. "Now you are going to find out," he added, and closing the door to the cage locked it.

The Red Umbrella

In the morning rush hour, a man in office clothes runs down the hill toward the station holding above his head a red umbrella. As the man hurries downhill he stops from time to time to wave with his free hand to the people who have stopped to wave to him. There is nothing unusual in all this waving, it happens every day, for the man with the red umbrella is well-known to us. What is unusual is the umbrella, for it is not raining. Nor is anyone else carrying such a device even to ward off the possible thought of a storm. But the man with the red umbrella continues to wave to the people waving back to him as he rushes down the hill, unaware of the absence of the rain as well as of the absence of umbrellas. And perhaps it is better so, we say, if the director of our local art museum does not see or feel what is going on around him today but simply continues dryly on his dark and downward way.

Holiday Season

We are building the Christmas crèche, as is our wont, during the holiday season, making everything life-size. "But there is no Child," says a child, looking into the manger. "Of course, there is no Child," we reply. "That is what we are waiting for, what we lack."

The Presentation

"I do not want to lose face," I said, walking into the bright rectangular room where he was to make the presentation, and feeling his own face stiffen even with the thought of what he had to say and do, insignificant as it was, as if this face of his were not a mask already, as if the mask, in a moment of revelation, could be removed.

Little Red

Little Red has lost her job. That is what we said, at first, at the office. We were wrong, once again, but that is what we said when we looked into her office and saw that she was not there. It was a windowless office, no larger than a closet. No wonder she is not there. I would be climbing the walls myself, we said. On what? a colleague asked, pointing out the obvious absence of anything like hand-holds or foot-holds in the office. There were no shelves, that was true. But bookshelves are for books, and what would a person like Little Red be doing with books? We had no idea what she did at the office, but reading was clearly not included in her job description. Perhaps she has not left the office, someone said. Perhaps she has gone on vacation. It cannot be a vacation, someone else said. She has not been here long enough to qualify for one. A sick day? The same, we said. Perhaps she has been promoted, said another. Perhaps she has been put in a higher office. That was possible, we said, but unlikely. What is it exactly that she does? What special skills are there in her skill set? No one knew. All we could do was stare into the empty space. Then one day it was not empty. There was a man there. He was a young man, we said, at least among ourselves, but not so young, we had to admit. He wore a black suit. A black suit and no tie. It lent him something of a wolfish appearance, we said. Would it not be better for his career if he varied his appearance? What kind of career can you expect a person in a windowless office to have, someone pointed out. Look what happened to Little Red. But of course we did not know what had happened to Little Red. We did not even remember her real name. Whatever it was, it was not Little Red. That much was sure. There was simply an empty space where a person had been, and then another person, altogether different. I can make nothing out of this story, someone said. On that we all agreed, as if, here at the office, even the last and least of narratives was being withdrawn from us.

From a Meeting of The Board

Committee Meeting, 31 October 2019, Members of the board present: Hamlet, The Frog Prince, Rumpelstilzchen, A. J. Prufrock, Cinderella, Hänsel and Gretel.

"I have called you here because, after careful examination of the political situation and its effect on the economy of our country," says the Frog Prince, "and a detailed comparison of the results of previous work with more recent developments, it is clear that if we are to advance and maintain our competitive edge we need more out-of-the-box thinking. The question is: How can recent developments in automation serve our own ends?"

"That is not the question," says Hamlet. "Need I remind you of our previous conclusions, or are we simply going to go on repeating the mistakes of the past *ad infinitum*?"

"We simply aren't being creative enough," admits Cinderella.

"We have robots for that," says Rumpelstilzchen. "A robot," he points out, "can work all day without needing sleep, lunch or coffee breaks. And it won't demand health care from the employer or add to the payroll tax burden."

"As a woman," Gretel interrupts, "I have a problem with the suppression of gender in your use of pronouns."

"I was referencing robots," retorts Rumpelstilzchen.

"I think you need to make that clearer."

"As a brother," begins Hänsel, I would like to side with my sister. But as a man – "

"You call yourself a man," says Rumpelstilzchen, unable to restrain himself. "Look at yourself. You are nothing but a character in a fairy tale."

"I am a transhumanist who hopes to achieve a prosthetic immortality by uploading his mind to a computer."

"Well put, brother," says Gretel. "I want to remind you that it is the economy that must invent new jobs and industries."

"Is that what you call out-of-the-box thinking?" asks the Frog Prince.

"Do not use that word in my presence," replies Gretel. "Remember what happened to the gingerbread house."

"Are we not talking of managerial feudalism," asks Rumpelstilzchen, trying to smooth the waters, "and the harmony that happens when economic and political narratives merge?"

"I understand the importance of transformational logic," says the Frog Prince.

"It is not harmony but disruption that we need," suggests A. J. Prufrock.

"Of course," replies Rumpelstilzchen. "For a higher harmony."

"That is not what I meant. That is not it, at all."

"For whom, and according to what?" asks Cinderella, reminding the board of her humble origins.

"We must never forget the pumpkin."

"This is not a halloween story," counters Hamlet.

"Who said it was?" replies Cinderella. "I was only speaking of how suddenly in this day and age expectations can collapse."

Musician of Silence

In my report I would like to make clear that when the woman in question decided to leave the office early one day she did so without my permission or that of anyone else, apparently assuming that, small as her office was, no one would look into her space, and if, for some reason, someone did look into the office and saw that it was empty, the emptiness would not be noted as anything out of the ordinary and for that reason would not be held against her. She was wrong, of course. We have our ways of knowing what is happening at the office, even if to all appearances nothing appears to be happening. Appearances can be deceptive, after all. Suffice it to say that in this particular case the office was empty and that this particular emptiness was observed and reported to her Nominal Superior: the new employee was not in her office, a clear violation of office policy in general and of our company rules in particular. It was her birthday, that is what we now know, and from the woman herself, and since it was her birthday she had decided that she would treat herself that evening to a meal with friends that she would cook herself. So she left the office early, as stated above, justifying her wayward behavior first to herself and later to her Superior with the argument, absurd as it may sound, that if at work there is no work then there is no reason for a person to remain at work. She was efficient, that is true, efficient and altogether competent at the tasks which she was given to perform, and, as a result of her competence and efficiency, she often found herself in the position of a person having nothing to do at the office. That, she claims, was the situation on the day in question, and so, for the first time in her life, she left the office early. She bought her groceries and was crossing the Park when, in broad daylight, a man put a knife to her throat and forced her down between some bushes on the path she had been following. I want to point out that most of us here at the office do not cross the Park even in broad daylight, but she was a country girl and no doubt had a need of the occasional tree. She screamed, but no one came to her rescue. She fought, but cut her hands on the knife. This is why she has not been able to type since the unfortunate incident. She claims to have asked for something else to do, something as simple as manning the telephones, but she has been informed correctly that such a shift in responsibilities would violate her job description and is thus out of the question. That is how the situation now stands. She will lose her job, she must lose her job, that much is clear, we have our principles, our policies. I would like to point out that the young woman in question continues to come to the office each morning, even if with her hands in bandages she is now incapable of performing the tasks assigned to her. All she does is to sit at her desk all day and hold her hands above the keyboard of her typewriter, as if she were a musician, waiting for the silence to begin.

The Whole Story

One day, after office hours, so runs the story, our department secretary went to the copying machine. There is certainly nothing out of the ordinary about a person going to a copying machine, young or old, male or female. How often had she gone to the copying machine? How often has any of us gone to the copying machine? Who can count the ways? But this time something out of the ordinary happened, so people say: the young woman – and she is not an unattractive young woman, that is certainly the consensus among the men on our team – apparently made a copy of herself. That is the story, at any rate, the whole story. Unbelievable, but true, so I am told. She is an efficient office worker, I should add, she has always performed her tasks to our complete satisfaction, and so even now it is impossible for me for a moment to think that she could accidentally have left a copy of her print-out in the machine. But that is what people say, and the next morning everything was brought to the attention of her immediate superior. I have no idea how he identified the woman. Perhaps he submitted all the female employees in our company to an interview. Perhaps the woman herself confessed to what she had done. There are even some at our office who claim that the woman in question admitted to the act with pride, as if such an act were in itself a statement, a form of protest, the whole story.

Relics

It is nothing, in reality, what you hold in your hands, or next to nothing, the skeleton of a sea-bird, a few bleached lines abandoned to the beach, a kind of cuneiform, in a way, only in reverse, not scratched into stone but carved by rock into bone, or what is left of rock at the edge of the sea, no more than sand, the former flight only to be imagined now, bone diagram of what once was: messenger of another time, another dimension, angelic reminder, ancient annunciation. For once, then, something.

Coda for Unaccompanied Silence

The Rock

There it is, I thought, looking at the island isolated in the sea, that is the family rock, the castle, what remains of it: a breeding place for the birds. Gannets, he told himself, looking more closely. Gannets is what he had read, gannets it would have to be. And to think that the King once sent his young son there to be kept in safety from the storming armies, that your own blood once flowed and failed in the royal veins, that once upon a time that waste of rock was given to the family in return for services rendered to the Conqueror, fierce warriors that we were in those first days, inheritors now dispossessed of what possessed us once. Is it not wonderful, I thought, looking out at the distant smudge, is it not wonderful to look out now at the ancestral home that became a prison and is now a ruin and to see the birds like words fleck off into the sky, wings wide upon the wind.

Mail Room

There is no denying his fame, though most of us no longer have the time or leisure to recall the images once reproduced the whole world over; the fleshy female on the back of the bull, her head turned back in fear and terror at what awaits her as the old consistencies of *terra firma* slip and slide underfoot and the beast, head haloed in the garland she has given him, plunges into the rough, oblivious sea. But times have changed, we want to say. If such an image can still grace the walls of our museums, no doubt it is to show our children and grandchildren the violence we come from and have overcome. I do not know what happened to the woman in the picture, if anything; we have no women in our top positions here, and the cleaning ladies work alone at night. But I sometimes see the old divinity alone in the mail room, too old to work efficiently, but not yet able to retire, distributing the mail, and nothing left of triumph but a smirk.

Receptionist

We have hired a giraffe as our receptionist. Why, you ask. Why not, we answer. Think of the advantages. Think of the quiet, the reserve. Think of the height. Even the President is nothing next to him. All our receptionist must do to see who is working or not working is to look – no need to leave the desk, no need even to stretch a neck. Of course, there has been criticism, and from the start, from those who still oppose diversity. But not within our ranks. We are after all a multinational corporation, our organization must reflect the world in which we live. But the costume, critics say. A gangster suit. From a fashionable designer, we point out, a well-known art collector and philanthropist. The ethnic background, they object. What ethnic background, we reply. The days of ethnic backgrounds are long gone. Look at the giraffe. Born in this country but of parents from abroad. So what if his progenitors were forced to move from place to place? Do you know nothing of the history of Europe or of Africa? Have you not seen the refugees? Dwarfs we may be, at least here at the office, compared to the giraffe. But that is all the more reason for us to have someone to look up to at our work.

Paris in the Age of Contagion

The young are dawdling, showing off their youth, only the old are in a hurry, avoiding each other, keeping their distance. Down at the river's edge my sycamore of more than fifty years has been torn down – a sapling in a cage now has the dirt. I hurry on without a goal. The city inside out. Wall after wall. The cafés closed, the restaurants, the theatres, circuses, museums, schools, businesses. No bird song on the sidewalks, no kisses on the cheeks. Only at a wrought-iron grill that barricades a courtyard from the world has a crowd of all ages begun to form: two street musicians, one singer, one guitar, making music as if their lives depended on it.

The Room

Once life was simple. I had my castle, and you had yours. At night I could ride over to your place, or you to mine, and that was that. How rich the darkness then, how solitary, how divine! But now the old frontier divides us once again, and the new rules of confinement and quarantine make it impossible for either one of us to reach the other. All we can do to re-create our trysts and trust is to meet at the one inn in the village through which the border passes, you from your country, I from mine, and spend the night together in the only room that straddles both lands, you on your side of the bed, and I on mine, in the hope that if there are no laws to keep the law at bay then there are still forms of politeness, customs if not traditions. Who cares if we must now reserve the room weeks if not months in advance, who cares if we have to tip-toe separately down the corridors of separate nations, who cares if in a time of contagion, love has become not only a risk but a crime as long as we have the courage to commit it?

Casting Now

Dust was falling over everything when a man no longer young but not yet altogether old arrived at the place he had sought for so long. Looking into the distance he could see that it was a convoy of trucks that was leaving the dust behind them in their wake. There were no people anywhere except for a few workmen and workwomen dismantling what looked like rows of street signs. The new arrival watched in fascination as the names were separated from the metal posts and piled into the rear of one pick-up truck after another and then driven away until only the posts remained in place, and then, one after another, they, too, were taken down and driven off. Only one truck remained in place, motionless in the dust storm and much smaller than the others. That must be the ticket office, the new arrival told himself, mistakenly, before he came closer and could make out the words:

Casting Now

So I have come to the right place after all, he told himself, and did his best to hurry to the window, as if, should he not hurry now, it, too, would disappear in a cloud of dust. For some reason, the window had been barred and behind the bars sat a man much older than himself, as old as he might hope to be one day, if all went well, a book propped open on the desk in front of him, looking at what appeared to be nothing more substantial than a series of horizontal lines.

"I have come here for an audition."

"What experience do you have?" said the other, not raising his eyes from the book.

"None whatsoever," he had to admit, "at least not in the professional theatre. But in my life – "

"I only ask," said the other, interrupting him, "because experience is not what we are looking for. The more experience, the more difficulty people have adapting to new roles. At least that has been our experience here.

"But I'm sorry to say," the man at the window went on, "that you have come too late. All the parts, for the moment at least, have been distributed."

"Or too early," the younger said, and tried to smile.

"If I could speak to the Director," he went on, "perhaps we could arrange a later date for an audition."

"There is no Director," the man at the window replied. "The role of the Director was abolished long ago."

"If I could see a script, then, so that I could prepare myself…."

"There is no script. That, too, has been abolished. That is what makes our theatre so unique. No performance is ever the same. No performance can be."

"Then why is everyone in such a hurry to leave?"

"Haven't you heard?" the other answered. "Gatherings of more than five people are now prohibited. Otherwise, I might have offered you a place in the audience. But it is the audience itself that has been abolished.

"It is the social distancing," the old man continued, as if reading his thoughts. "That is why there is no one in the trucks, except for the drivers, of course, there are only the sets and props and costumes. Though you can see that couples are allowed to ride their bicycles abreast. That is a solution that works for the moment, though in the long run, obviously, it will pose a problem. Look for yourself."

The younger man looked as directed and saw that the vehicles appeared to stretch into the distance forever. He would have thought such trucks and trailers more appropriate for a circus and its animals than for the people in a theatre. All the members of the company, or what he took to be the members of the company, were on bicycles, riding one after another, except for the couples bicycling abreast. It was a travelling theatre, that much he knew, but he would have thought that precisely because it was a travelling theatre even in such times as these they would have found a more efficient mode of transportation.

"There must still be a need for people," he suggested, "if only to sell tickets."

"You do not understand," said the other. "This is not a commercial venture. Here every person who would like to be a part of the experience automatically becomes a member of the company even if we have no roles for that person at the moment and they must simply watch and wait. Even if they have no role they are as observers part of the performance, perhaps the most important part of all."

"What, then, can I expect?"

"To wait," the other said.

"I have been waiting all my life."

"Then you must know that that, too, is a form of work."

With these words the old man slowly began to close the book in front of him, as if that in itself were an accomplishment, and then drew down the shade behind the window.

"For by your work," he added, from behind the shade, "you shall be known."

On the Flying Trapeze

The beautiful young woman on the flying trapeze is coming to our town, that is what all the posters say, that is why we are here, all of us, in the public square, waiting for the artist to arrive; and when she does, surrounded by her trainers, we who have never seen her, famous though she has become, we who have only read of her furious flights, first and foremost are surprised by how small the person is, no larger nor more muscular than any other woman in the crowd, though dressed extraordinarily, we must admit, in brief military fatigues ringed round by the gossamer skirt of a ballerina. She is not young, we can see that at once, we who have never seen her, and since our ideas of beauty somehow still depend on youth even as we age it is impossible for us to say that the beautiful young woman on the flying trapeze is actually beautiful. She has had a hard life, that much we can say, that much we can see in the lines of her face, love and loss, we say, are etched into the flesh, she has known both, clearly, and hardship, too, much like ourselves. And here she is, now, among us, being lifted by a crane into the air above our heads on her trapeze, higher and higher, bowing to the crowd below. She is still very good at bowing, that is something she has not lost, making grand theatrical gestures from her perch on high, though when she begins to practice her art it is clear, at least to some, and not only to those who remember the days of glory, that things are not now what they once were or might have been. Some of us close our eyes, then, preferring to imagine the arcs in air, and perhaps it is better so, we say, if only to ourselves, at such a moment, to consider the trajectory of a woman not in space alone but in time as well, arcing from here to there, from this to that, precariously balanced if balanced at all, the actual arc invisible in fact but for the imagination.

Circus Animals

One's initial impression at a circus may be of an almost infinite number of artists, but if you have ever gone behind the scenes and looked among the cages you know that in reality there are only a few; each must play many roles, and not just in a lifetime, but in a single day. The economics of necessity require nothing less, the fundamental poverty underlying even the most glamorous of performances forces the performers, once their individual moment under the arc lights is over, into mutual cooperation, and once the show has ended the real work only begins. The clowns, invariably people whose talent refuses to fit into any particular skill, usually end up with the odd jobs. The beautiful young women serve the food. Even the mighty ringmaster with his whip and stool has other duties, for we circus performers insist on preserving some mark of our fundamental equality, even if it is only a shared humiliation, and so the ringmaster is traditionally found sitting behind the bars of the box office, dispensing tickets to whoever is willing to pay. The trapeze artists themselves, the most glorious of artists, have the most dismal and degrading of secondary jobs: to look after the cages. From them arises the most atrocious smell, even more intense on the days of a double performance. Then extra food must be placed between the bars, buckets readied for the added excrement, some of the animals, the more cunning, realizing what a bad day awaits them, refuse to eat; then food has actually to be stuffed down their throats. They who have held the most delicate of bars, and then let everything go, flying through nothing but air, knowing all alone the bliss of freedom, as the crowd gasps, lowering their eyes, and not only in terror, but also to be ready for the moment if and when the artist should fail, must now on earth carry buckets filled with shit. And although it is a service to the other animals, they are despised and even scorned, as though the food and decency and even the order they provide were unwanted in what is after all a life in captivity. The big cats are the worst: they snarl at the artists as they pass with their brushes and brooms, making threatening gestures, pacing back and forth, like the most powerful of people in their offices, and these threatening noises are transformed to the lesser cats, the panthers and the leopards that, should you come too close, would just as thoroughly kill you. Such is the fate of the trapeze artist. These degradations and humiliations only make them yearn for the open air. There, on the ladder once more, knowing what it is to what they must come down, they dream of even more daring and dangerous feats: many bars are needed now, each set in motion, each let go, and in a rhythm all their own, releasing now this one and now that, until the bars themselves become mere lines of reference, themselves flying through space, now here, and then, nowhere.

And there are people who have no other task but to repair the tents, sewing up the holes that inevitably appear in the texture of things. Perhaps the day will come when a special light will be known, a light that needs no background, to show the human figure, and then circuses will be held in the open, somewhere in the world the animals will be let loose, at least some of these odious jobs will be dispensed with and the trapeze artists will not have to practice their art under the humiliating limitation of a canvas ceiling, rigged by others, but can swing freely among the stars.

You and I

I must be called up for military service. Why I, I asks. Why not, we answer. Someone must be called. Someone must be ready in case there is a war. And there is always a war. We have been at war for as long as I can remember. Even when we are not at war, officially, there is a war, a secret war, a war we do not dare declare for fear of losing it. Thus the secrecy. Thus the registration of every male citizen of this country at the age of eighteen. Why not every female citizen as well, you ask. Is that not something we should all be fighting for? Are we not after all a society of equals, at least potentially? Why not include the female, too? Because someone must stay home, we say, if home itself is to stay home. I can not understand the finer points of logic, so it seems. What is there to defend, I wants to know, here and not there, if what is here is different from what is there? Freedom, we reply. If I were free, I would not be here, I says. Think of the little woman, we reply. What woman, I says. The one not here, we answer. The ones not here. Think of all the ones not here. The ones at home. There is no one at home, I says. Those days are gone forever. Wait and see, we say. No one can say for sure what the future will bring. You do not understand, I says. A person is a world. And if I kill another person, if I even agree to kill another person, I destroy the world. And for what? A world that's predicated on the destruction of the world? But think of everything that you will gain, we answer, if only you survive. That, from a moral point of view, says I, only makes everything worse.

Bread and Circuses

There are people who refuse to accept the dwarf at the circus to-day, people who for that reason refuse to attend even a single performance. But why this opposition to the dwarf? We are all used to the sight of the ringmaster behind bars, selling tickets to the show before a performance, we are all used to the presence of beautiful young women serving food at intermission, we are all used to the speed of the most aerial of acrobats dispensing drinks to the crowd after a performance. These secondary jobs are an inevitable part of an artist's life, and we all know and accept this without protest or complaint. But dwarfs? A dwarf has no real job, no purpose, our critics argue, but to greet the crowd – as if that were not work enough. A dwarf does nothing but delight the children. Moreover, they object, look at the make-up and the costumes: such bright and cheerful colors, as if to disguise the essential tragedy and thus strew illusion in the eyes of children. Of course, this is only the beginning, this talk of dwarfs. Already there is a movement underway to get rid of the animals as well, and in the name of rights, though where the animals would go is a question animal rightists prefer to avoid: after a career in the circus would not confinement in a zoo be the ultimate degradation, at least from the animal point of view, a life deprived of special skills, even of the possibility of learning anything new; and as to a life out in the open, our animals, domesticated as they have become, would not survive. And once the animals go, the animal trainers will also cease to exist. And what about the clowns? They, too, will disappear. Only the acrobats will remain. But who will rig the ropes and ladders, then? Even now, in spite of the lip service still paid to us, in spite of the occasional honors, the long years of training required for the simple exercise of our talents make it next to impossible for emerging artists to acquire even the most rudimentary of skills, not to mention the rising costs of education. Many of our younger aspirants, especially those of modest means, now have to go abroad to seek their schooling, but once abroad, even if furnished finally with the finest of diplomas, and from the most famous of finishing schools, find themselves considered no better than traitors by the authorities at home. Is it any wonder, then, that we at the circus protest each and every incursion into our realm, each and every erasure of the traditions that have made us what we are, that we point out to our critics, such as they are, that, if there have always been bread and circuses, in our time it does not follow that there always will be. Man does not live by bread alone, nor woman, either, we point out, but once the circus goes the bread will vanish, too.

Another Story

1

Cinderella put on her new designer jeans, the blue ones with the tears already worked into the fabric, stepped into what still looked like a carriage, gave the coachman instructions for the journey, and then set off on her way.

She was looking for a story, another story, any story but her own, which had already begun to bore her, brief as it was.

She had soon put the house behind her as well as the village and now the unfamiliar world of rocks and trees appeared to disappear in front of her.

Then there was a crash, as of a pumpkin breaking, and the vehicle, such as it was, came to a stop.

"Why don't you come out of your ivory carriage?" said a voice from outside.

"It is not made of ivory," Cinderella answered, tartly.

"You are avoiding the question," replied the wolf. "If you want to get out of the story, that is the only way. One is not princess a hundred yards from the carriage, as I'm sure you know."

"I am not a princess," the young woman replied. "I am not even a duchess. I have had a hard life, if you really want to know."

"What can you know of hardship, at your age?" the wolf replied, and in his voice the young woman detected something sad and wistful, even noble, as if he himself in reality were not a wolf but a prince in disguise.

"Do you really want to hear my family story? My mother – "

"What you need is a grandmother, not a mother or a step-mother," said the wolf, smartly. "And I know a very nice one, all alone, in a house in the woods."

"Is it made of gingerbread?" the young woman asked.

"No," said the wolf.

"Then it is not for me."

2

In the distance the trees had been burnt and twisted out of shape, those few remaining rooted to the earth now had the look of letters black against the sky.

There was the sound of gunfire, then silence, then gunfire again.

People were crying beside the road, women and children, in small groups, no doubt families, those no longer able to walk carried on the shoulders of others.

The sight of so much suffering hurt the young woman. She closed her eyes, and thought of the sky somewhere else, blue and beautiful.

Abruptly, everything came to a stop. Something must have interrupted the progress of the vehicle.

Cinderella opened her eyes, but before she could think of anything, she saw that seven soldiers in camouflage had surrounded the carriage.

In spite of their guns, if not because of them, the soldiers appeared smaller than the idea she thought she had had of men in uniform.

"Your passport, please," said the largest, apparently an officer.

"I have no passport."

"You have no passport and you travel abroad?"

"This is not a foreign country, at least not for me. My father – "

"You are in another story and every story is a foreign country, no matter how familiar it might first appear. Haven't you learned a thing in all your reading?"

"I do not read to learn," the young woman replied, not without a touch of pride, "though I fail to see what my attitude toward narrative art has to do with the likes of you."

At that moment a woman Cinderella had not seen began to cry out something from a miniature house on the hill she had not noticed. Turning toward the miniscule door Cinderella at once recognized Snow White.

"What is Snow White doing in a place like this?" she asked the smallest of the soldiers, who had a moustache that distinguished him from the others.

"Working for us. Cooking, cleaning, caring – you name it, it gets done! What a lucky girl you are! She has just finished making us our dinner, so we'll have to let you go. For to be late for such a meal would be a discourtesy for which not one of us could ever be forgiven, not by Snow White, not by you, not even by ourselves."

3

Office buildings rose into the distance at long last, blocking out the sun and casting what remained of the road in long lines of blankness and obscurity. It looked as if the shadows of the buildings had been bent and folded back upon their sources, having no other place to go. But she was not going to complain at this moment in the story. What she wanted now was a position of her own. After all, at the end of the day, she did not need a carriage or a castle. In the final analysis, she did not need a passport or identity papers. And if push came to shove, she did not even need a man. All men were wolves, anyway. At least at some point in time. All men were dwarfs. At least at some moment in life. And if she ever needed a companion, she could buy herself a dog. At any rate, where she was going there were no longer any wolves. There were no longer any fairy tales. Even the name of Cinderella was a fiction. It was only a way of speaking.

My Own Star

1

"What are you going to do?" asks the father.

"Are you going to be a doctor or a lawyer?"

"Neither," says the son. "I am going to follow my own star."

"Then you can follow your own star," the father replies, "right out the door of this house."

2

"I am going to live life lyrically."

"And what does that mean?" asks the mother.

"That there will be measure in everything," the son replies. "When I am young, that will be the time to be young. And when I am old, that will be the time to be old."

"And you call that a plan?"

3

Stars are slipping from the sky, showering the darkness like spring rain.

"What will you do if your star falls?"

"Look for another."

"Aren't you the optimist!" says the young woman.

"Do you know what an optimist is?" the young man replies. "A person who has had to spend life with a pessimist."

"And a pessimist?"

"The opposite."

Chamber of Culture

The question of culture, of what is culture and what not, has become a divisive issue in our time, especially when it comes to public funding, limited as our resources inevitably are, and so we have appointed U as Custodian of The National Trust and put The Trust in charge of The Intellectual and Spiritual Education of the People. We have created the Ancestral Heritage House, an office where you can trace the genetic history of each and every citizen and non-citizen alike. We have also established a Chamber of Culture, modeled on the Chamber of Commerce, in each and every one of our important cities, an important city being one which by definition includes a Chamber of Culture, for man does not live by bread alone, and we are now in the process of replacing the local critics with our own experts who, in future, will have the task of deciding which of our citizens will be permitted to be recognized as artists and which not. As an additional proof of our concern for culture, we have set up local Committees for the Assessment of Inferior Work. Aware as we are that values can and do change, and not only in the world of art, and thus the concept of value itself, members of the Committee have been instructed to safeguard those works which have been confiscated for possible future use. As soon as these procedures prove effective, we shall set up similar processes for the written word and, by implication, the unwritten word as well. With these measures we are convinced that a final solution will be found, one that will cleanse the nation not only of what have become unnecessary questions, but also of the question of necessity itself.

In the Ruins and Rubble

No one recognizes the woman attempting with her bare hands to bury her brother in the dirt. No one recognizes the authorities, either, as they move among us in disguise watching us as we honor the dead, forbidden as it is. This is our duty, we say, if we say anything. But do not take everything so seriously, say the authorities, in the future you will have our roles and if not tomorrow as soon as you have learned how to act properly. It may be only an act for you, we reply, if we reply at all, but the show goes on. We will not be denied. We have crossed the waters, those of us who have not drowned, we are all Antigones now, each and every one of us, digging in the dirt.

The Wrong Story

She was in the wrong story, that much was clear, that much had been clear right from the beginning. But what was the right story, if there was a story at all? And who would tell it – and to whom – if not herself, if it was to be her story? Why should there be a story, anyway? After all, the day had begun like any other: she had awakened to the noise of construction opposite her bedroom, opened the slats of the shutters once again, once again looked out through the gaps even though she knew what she was going to see, and once she had seen it, the construction site, paddled into the kitchen to prepare a cup of tea. Even on her way to work, dressed now in the clothes she would soon exchange for others, nothing out of the ordinary had happened. She entered the workplace as she always did, aware once again that the mirrors could as easily be office walls, that the absence of people here at this time of day could as easily be the absence of people somewhere else in the world. It was not what she had imagined that she would be doing, that was the thing, what she was doing now, before one thing led to another, as one thing will, and you were here and nowhere else, removing all the layers that had no other purpose but to be removed. So it is with striptease: the creative part of the dance is not what you take off, it is what you put on. And so it is with a story: if its loss is of any significance, it is only what you have to lose.

Classical Balance

Odysseus went down into the Underworld to speak with his mother, Aeneas to speak with his father, so that taken together a classical balance was achieved, one that left nothing for later generations to do. At least that is the opinion of scholars today. Thus they should not object if we simply leave the old ones alone. Let them dissolve into the silence, let them return to a time before we were born, let them meet again without a single thought of ourselves.

The Metaphysics of Mountain Climbing

Little has been made of the metaphysics of mountain climbing, and with good reason, we say, for the mountain is not only a monument to the desire of each and every climber but also its utter annihilation. Let the golden-mean people content themselves with half-way measures. We climbers lose our purpose in attaining it. We rise as we create our own abyss – and then do what we can to come down to it.

Clouds

A young black woman stands in an abandoned cotton field looking at the clouds as they drift across a telephone line. They look like
sheep leaping over a strand of electrified wire, she tells herself. White
sheep, of course, she adds, with a laugh. What can they know of being
fair or free, watching the forms as they dissolve in air.

Bird Watching

I saw it first at night. For some reason I was walking alone along the rocks and shells and sea-weed of the Sound in the darkness. I did a lot of walking in the darkness in those days – in those days there seemed to be a lot of darkness to get through, as if you could get through it if only you continued long and far enough. And then there it was: a slim white vertical, a silent exclamation mark that brought the steps to a sudden stop. It was low tide. The bird was standing in the shallows of an island that at other times did not exist. In the darkness it appeared to glow with the mystery of a revelation still to come. Somehow I thought of a long-leggèd reading lamp and simultaneously of a woman's body, though at that time I had still to see a woman without clothes and I did not yet have a reading lamp of his own. The night bird was a presence in which the future was to have a place, but not the past, clearly, at least as far as I could tell, for at that moment there was only the egret in the darkness ahead, the egret and no regret. Now so many years later – years of darkness and of light – there it is, again, the bird, but now far from the Sound, far from the country and the continent I used to call his own, immobile in a farmer's field, searching for something in the silence as the car speeds by.

Woman at the Window

You have fallen in love, that is what people say, and if you have not soon you will, and if not soon some day. For we all fall in love. But why the word fall? Why do we fall? Why do we have to fall? What do we have to fall from, anyway? What does anyone have to fall from? And if we fall is it not like the snow, I thought, watching the first of winter from the window, this falling and rising that I feel? For the snow falls only to rise again, higher and higher, changing everything, and with the least, the lightest, of all touches, making even the branches of the trees look brighter, blacker and cleaner in the growing light. It must be like love, then, whatever love is, this falling through the night. And if in the morning, or later, nothing remains except what you can remember, remember: the earth has been enriched, the rivers run again.

Susanna and the Elders

When Susanna was surprised by the elders in the garden at her bath, it was the two old men who were accused of violating the privacy of the young woman and not the woman theirs. We know the published version of the story: the elders, thwarted in desire, claimed to have discovered Susanna in the act of adultery, and so it was the woman who was convicted of the sin that the men were said to have hoped to commit with her. But separated from each other after the trial, the two old men could not agree on what had happened, their lack of agreement was taken as proof that at least one of them was lying, and in the interest of society if not of justice both were put to death, so that Susanna in her innocence was now guilty of having helped to violate the ancient and divine commandment not to kill. But anyone who has looked long and carefully at the picture, the only living testimony that we have today of the crime, and compared the fountain and the flesh, can see that it could equally have been the water that the two old men were regarding, old as they were, the water and the rock, and not the woman, beautiful as she was or might have been, and with the fervor of Hosanna.

In the Hospital

"Our love has grown perfect," Alexander says, "or as close to perfect as anything can be in this world, except for the fact that we have to die." "But then," Bucephalus answers, with a snort, from the next bed, "if we did not have to die, our love would never have been born in the first place."

Exercise

"I don't know! I just don't know," I cried out, jogging around the circular cinder track and doing what I could to concentrate not on the water at the center but on the words above the office buildings rising in the distance above the trees. "What is it you don't know?" my companion cried, a step behind me, short of breath as he inevitably was. "I don't know," I cried back. "Even that I don't know."

In a Class by Themselves

"I am an unwritten page," says the youngest of the three women, and thrusts forward her upper body so that it is impossible not to notice the button holes drawn tight. "I have a story," says the second, sadly, as if there were nothing worse for a human being to admit in life. "I am the story," says the third, brazenly, the oldest of the three, and the one, in spite of the words, if not because of them, the most difficult to read.

Sign on a Wall

It is forbidden to place a sign here

Dwarf Trilogy

1. The Appearance of the Dwarf

The dwarf is said to measure six feet tall, but only with shoes on.

2. Documentary Evidence

A certain shrinkage is inevitable, report the doctors.

3. The Disappearance of the Dwarf

I have only appeared to disappear, says the dwarf.

Metaphor

The fly sits on the swatter, as if that were the best way to survive, so close to the deadly weapon that it cannot be used against him.

Words For the Wall

"Why did you let me go? Why did you give me up?"
That is the sort of thing a single person says to the wall.

Coming and Going

"Do not mind me, Madame. I am only the burglar."
"What have you taken?"
"Nothing."
"Then I must ask you to leave at once."
"Would you mind if I fetch my jacket before I go?"

A Logical Encounter

"You are no princess, and I am no prince. Is it not time, finally, for us, to treat each other simply as the ordinary human beings that we are?" "How, in that case, can you expect me to find you extraordinary?" "Or I you, for that matter?" "Would it not then be better, or at least more logical, if we simply continued on our separate ways?"

Wordstalk

The giant has been slain: that is the end of the story. Jack did the deed, our Jack, or so Jack says. Each day the boy went to the market with the cow, the only animal left on the farm, that much we saw with our own eyes, each day he came home to his mother with whatever he could get in trade for fresh milk, and then one day poor Jack came back without the cow. All he had to show for his efforts was a handful of beans. He was not much at business, we agreed. How could he be, we argued, in his favor, with no father in the house to teach him how to cut a deal, and as for money that a boy could practice with alone in that house there was none. Beans for a cow, the only animal they had – not much of a deal, we had to admit, even those of us who took his side. Not ordinary beans, Jack claimed. Magic beans! His mother in her rage threw them out the window and sent poor Jack to bed without his dinner, not that he missed much in that house. Everyone knows what Jack said happened next. Up sprang the beanstalk, back behind the house, and higher than a beanstalk has a right to be, as if it had taken root in something other than the earth. That is no beanstalk, we said. Not the kind of beanstalk we know. That is a figment of your imagination. As if to prove us wrong, Jack said that very day he climbed the thing, and with such energy as if it were the way to heaven. Do not insult us in our faith, we said. Whatever the way to heaven might be on earth, one thing is certain: it is not a beanstalk. When he came back to town he had a hen, and that was all, an ordinary hen. We mocked him, then. Some of the farmers in the town even began to cluck and moo. And then the eggs began to come. What eggs! Once Jack got started he could not be stopped. Each day he came to us with something new, a gift, he said. From whom, we did not ask. We did not dare. Of course, he had to build a chicken coop to keep us from the hen. The beanstalk had to be enclosed. He had to hire guards to keep the people out. There was now money in the house, that much was clear. That was when the rumors began, nasty rumors, rumors of the castle in the air, and of the giant and his wife who lived together there and how Jack was a common thief. Small as he was, he claimed that he could hide in corners of the castle and escape the giant's wrath. He had his farmboy smell, of course, and it was his smell, he said, that drove the giant into fits of rage and even rhyme. It was the harp that put an end to everything. The harp was no less magical than the beans and could play itself, Jack claimed, and when he stole the giant's instrument the music that it made awoke the giant and the famous chase began: Jack head-first down the stalk, the giant step-by-step behind him, Jack's mother at the foot of the beanstalk with the axe in hand. Jack was accused of murder, Jack and his mother, and of theft, though since no corpse was ever found it came as no surprise to us in town that both Jack and his mother were acquitted. We who know Jack for the story-teller that he is no longer talk of the beanstalk but the wordstalk when we talk of him. There is no such thing as a giant, there can be no such thing as a giant, not in an age of dwarfs such as our own. The time of Titans is long gone, we point out, those of us who still remember the old tall tales, even if the village idiot continues to proclaim that it is the body of the giant that has been broken in our midst like bread and that we are the crumbs.

All the Stories

All the stories had been gathered together in the place where they were to be distributed. "So many," said one. "No more than necessary," said another. "One person, one story," said a third, "even if they forget them." "They have to forget them, that is why they have them in the first place," said the first, "so that they can live, or try to live, as if nothing had been written."

Homeward Bound

Sail out far enough in the world, it was once said, and you will fall off the earth into the abyss. Today we know that the abyss is everywhere – no need to travel far to find it or to fall. It is in each and every action we perform, and, if words are acts, then equally in what we say and do not say, in the silences we keep for ourselves as well as in those kept for or from us. The world is round, now, we tell ourselves; sail out far enough, and long enough, and you'll come home.

Notes for Narcissus

Narcissus was astonished to find himself so definite, so ringed by contours, such a creature of lines, he who in his own mind was always going out into things and losing himself among them: budding and birding with the trees, opening to the light, unburdening himself. There were also the recurrent floods of darkness, of course, the washes and the weight of night, erasures where, if such a person can exist at all, it is only in dream, a dream that presupposes, happily or unhappily, a dreamer. Look into the waters that you wear and imagine what I feel each day, Narcissus tells himself: another death, another dawn. What pleasure to survive!

A Day in the Country

They are sitting at a table outdoors in the shade when you arrive, the old divinities. A chair stands empty on the grass. Perhaps this is the place reserved for you, you think, and you alone, as you approach. For have you not walked all this way to join them here, and in the rain and snow as well as in the absence of the rain and snow? But what is that terrible noise? Is that all that remains of the heavenly strains? Is it not possible that they are simply people like yourself, talking with each other, people who have come all this way, and no matter the weather, simply to enjoy a day in the country?

Before and After

When the doorkeeper finally closed the door, extinguishing the bright and famous slash of light that had seemed to glow from within, if not to emanate from the structure itself, the old man who like so many before him had waited all his life to enter what was now closed to him forever suddenly found himself lighter, less obscure, as if the time lost if not wasted in waiting had been returned to him, freed of the great weight of hope that had made him submit like his predecessors to the doorkeeper in the first place. "A story," he said to himself, only in a whisper, as if he might be overheard talking to himself, and half expecting to see the doorkeeper at his feet. But there was no one there, only a wall, and a door that, if it had existed once, now, when closed, was indistinguishable from the wall, even from the darkness itself.

The Sands of Amsterdam

The city of Amsterdam has been built on sand. Its history, and a long and tumultuous history it has been, disputed though the written record still is, stands as a rebuke to those who believe that a city to survive must be built on rock and rock alone. Look at our city, we say, look at Amsterdam. Walk the canals and admire the lines; admire the water as you walk and the reflections on the water. Look into the windows of our apartments and admire how we still live as we have always lived, without shades or blinds, as proud of ourselves and of our furnishings as John Locke or Descartes in their day. Had such a city been erected on rock it would never have survived. That may be a traditional model for a city built upon a hill, but not for one constructed at if not below the level of the sea. We owe our survival here to what is beneath us, and what is beneath us here in Amsterdam are the shifting sands. Our city, from the red-light district to the enduring sights of our museums, stands on the sands as on the shoulders of a dancer: it sways as a dancer sways, sways but does not fall, and with each rising and subsiding of the tide, both above and below the surface, and from The Night Watch to what we now hold in our hands in the broadest of daylight, a piece of our foundations, the least of things, and no more than a word, a grain of sand.

The Living Stone

If every page that you have written were a stone one meter long and if each stone were laid down in a single and unbroken line, the line would not even reach to the next town. But what is there in the next town that you want to reach? Are not the people there much as the people here? And when have you ever really wanted to go there yourself? Why for that matter talk of stones one meter long? Is it the tombstone, possibly, that you hope to evoke? Is what you write so polished? So succinct? So monumental? Why one meter? Why not proclaim the local, what you know, not the cemetery but the living stone, the pebbles at the beach, the varied rocks within the river, always on the move, in their own time, each interrupted in their flow and bed, down to the most minimal grain of sand? Not to mention the bedrock and occasional outcrop of the hills and valleys, the boulders broken off from the mother lode, eroded and erased, tossed here and there, abandoned by the glaciers, worn and torn, the rock still buried in the earth, unseen, and still to surface, unwritten, free of any lines, at least as far as you can tell, and as real as the dirt beneath your feet.

A Country Priest

The wind howls. The night falls. The snow accumulates. The road becomes impassible. How could you have thought of driving to the house? You must leave the car. The road can take you no further. There is no road, the road has vanished. How could you not have noticed? Only the drifts remain, hollows. The vehicle will have to be abandoned. Go on foot, you will have to continue on foot. Will you find it again, the vehicle, when you return? Or will it, too, have vanished in the blizzard? How often you have loved the snow, the fall of it, the weight of almost nothing rising into something, erasing everything, or almost everything. But now you must make your way without markers. You see the light, you can still see the light, far off, from the house on the hill. You must reach the dying. But the snow is thickening. The light has gone out, the house has vanished. It is all you can do not to burst into song.

www.ingramcontent.com/pod-product-compliance
Lightning Source LLC
Chambersburg PA
CBHW050802190726
48285CB00005B/1762